Evie was on the   back to say perhaps this wasn't a good idea, when he swept into the coffee shop.

He looked completely out of place among the groups of chatting mothers, phone-obsessed teens and crossword-filling pensioners. With his slicked-back hair, long wool coat and his handsome dark looks, he looked as though he'd just stepped out of an aftershave ad.

Even her heart gave a little gasp at the sight of him, and she knew why he was here. To concoct a fake relationship because he was too busy to entertain the idea of a real one. Not exactly the stuff dreams were made of but what she needed right now.

Evie gulped her chocolate, wishing for something more than cream and marshmallows to steel her for this encounter. He looked even more handsome and out of her league in daylight, and she wondered how the hell they were going to fool anyone into thinking they were a couple.

Dear Reader,

It's that time of year again! Christmas trees, fairy lights, hot chocolate and Christmas shopping—these are a few of my favorite things. All of which are in plentiful supply in my latest festive romance. Throw in some pottery classes, a fake-dating site and a daft dog, and hopefully you have the ideal book to curl up with on a cold winter's day.

Merry Christmas!

Karin xx

CINDERELLA'S
FESTIVE FAKE DATE

KARIN BAINE

ROMANCE

Harlequin®
ROMANCE

ISBN-13: 978-1-335-21620-5

Cinderella's Festive Fake Date

Copyright © 2024 by Karin Baine

Recycling programs for this product may not exist in your area.

Harlequin Enterprises ULC
22 Adelaide St. West, 41st Floor
Toronto, Ontario M5H 4E3, Canada
www.Harlequin.com

Printed in U.S.A.

Karin Baine lives in Northern Ireland with her husband, two sons and her out-of-control notebook collection. Her mother and her grandmother's vast collection of books inspired her love of reading and her dream of becoming a Harlequin author. Now she can tell people she has a *proper* job! You can follow Karin on X @karinbaine1 or visit her website for the latest news, karinbaine.com.

Books by Karin Baine

Harlequin Romance

Pregnant Princess at the Altar
Highland Fling with Her Boss

Harlequin Medical Romance

Royal Docs

Surgeon Prince's Fake Fiancée
A Mother for His Little Princess

Wed for Their One Night Baby
A GP to Steal His Heart
Single Dad for the Heart Doctor
Falling Again for the Surgeon
Nurse's Risk with the Rebel
An American Doctor in Ireland
Midwife's One-Night Baby Surprise
Festive Fling with the Surgeon

Visit the Author Profile page
at Harlequin.com for more titles.

With thanks to Helen for sharing her pottery skills.

For Sheva xx

Praise for
Karin Baine

"Emotionally enchanting! The story was fast-paced, emotionally charged and oh so satisfying!"

—*Goodreads* on *Their One-Night Twin Surprise*

CHAPTER ONE

'Nope. No way. Absolutely no chance in hell. N-O!'

Evie didn't know how else she could say it. There was no way she was going to go home to spend the evening with her stepfamily when she'd done her best to avoid them as much as she could for the past few years.

'Don't you go home every year for the annual switching on of the family Christmas lights? I mean, according to you it's a six-foot plastic tree with some fairy lights strung round it, so I don't know what the big deal is, but you usually participate.'

Ursula, Evie's studio assistant, rested her head in her hands, elbows on the workbench, watching her at the pottery wheel.

'Under duress, and it's the only time I usually visit. This is different. It's not just putting on a happy face and gritting my teeth in front of Courtney and Bailey. This is to celebrate their engagement. How am I supposed to get through that without bawling, or finally telling them that they're two-faced back-stabbing traitors who don't deserve to have me in their lives?'

The anger she'd been suppressing for too long seemed to work its way through her body and out of her fingertips, until she was strangling the clay vase she'd been lovingly and delicately shaping until then. The clay wobbled and collapsed, leaving her no option but to take her foot off the pedal to stop the wheel and scrap her work. She tossed it into the bucket with the other remnants for recycling later, and it landed with a satisfying wet slap. What she wouldn't do to toss her stepsister and ex-boyfriend in there along with it.

'I vote for the second option. It's been a long time coming. Honestly, I don't know how you've stayed in contact at all. I would've flipped my lid by now.'

Ursula lifted a ball of new clay and plonked it in the centre of the wheel for her, though Evie knew it was pointless trying to work now. It would be impossible to concentrate on lovingly creating something beautiful to sell at the potters' Christmas market coming up when she was so full of pent-up rage.

She wiped her hands on her apron and turned off the wheel. 'It wouldn't achieve anything. I'd be accused of being overdramatic and selfish. I'll just seethe in private.'

If it had been anyone else, she would've severed all ties and got on with her own life. To some extent she'd probably done just that, setting up her own studio in the heart of Belfast and focusing on her work. However, Courtney, her stepsister, was the only family she had left, other than her stepmother. With no one else in her life apart from Ursula, and her other, hairier, studio assistant, Dave the golden retriever, abandoning her family didn't seem like a viable option.

Besides, she'd promised her father on his deathbed to keep their family together, to be tolerant of her stepsister, who, even fifteen years ago, had been a princess, someone incapable of taking anyone's feelings into account other than her own. Evie's father had obviously witnessed some of her stepmother's favouritism towards her own daughter, over the one she'd inherited with her husband. Perhaps he'd hoped it would lessen over the years, that they would grow closer, never imagining that his child would be treated as a lodger, a burden, in the wake of his death.

When she looked at it like that, Evie wondered why she did bother keeping in touch at all. Deep down, she knew it was only because they were the last connection she had to her father, and she had a promise to keep.

None of which would make it any easier to stomach a return to 'celebrate' this painful engagement, and reminder of betrayal.

Ursula screwed up her face. 'It's not healthy bottling everything up. What you need is closure. Wave them off on their life together, and walk away.'

'Which is all well and good in theory, but I don't want to end up a teary, snivelling mess in front of the smug twosome.'

Even thinking about it was making her stomach churn. Her stepmother fawning over the pair, Evie feigning happiness for them, and feeling outnumbered. On her own. As usual.

'Hmm. If you want, I'll come with you and give them a piece of my mind.'

The thought of firecracker Ursula letting rip and telling Courtney and Bailey how vile they were for treating her friend so appallingly did cheer Evie up. However, she knew it wasn't the solution. It would just be seen as spiteful on her part for putting a stranger up to it.

'I don't think that would be a good idea. Besides, I'm sure you have other, more exciting plans for a December weekend than watching fairy lights on a plastic tree being switched on.'

Her friend was the extrovert Evie wished she could be, who lived to the beat of her own drum and didn't give a hoot what anyone else thought.

'Well… I do have a hot date…'

'Naturally.'

There were very few Saturday nights when Ursula didn't have plans with a handsome man or, at the very least, a glamorous girls' weekend away somewhere expensive and indulgent. She was lucky she had Mummy and Daddy to fund that lifestyle, and a bulging little black book full of phone numbers from adoring men who couldn't seem to get enough of her.

All things elusive to Evie, who'd had to work hard for everything she did have. Although she wasn't in the market for any kind of relationship after Bailey had broken her heart. These days, the only man in her life was Dave. He wouldn't leave her for another woman. At least for as long as she kept cooking him sausages.

'I know! Why don't you join a dating site? You could take a man with you and stick two fingers up at Bailey and Courtney.' Ursula began scrolling through her phone. No doubt she was signed up to every dating app going. That was probably why she was never stuck for a date.

Evie, on the other hand, was averse to most modern technologies. She loathed social media in general but was forced to engage, posting content and selling online so her business could survive. Therefore, the idea of soulless dating apps based entirely on a person's appearance was her idea of hell. If she couldn't trust someone she'd known for years, basing a relationship on her attractiveness to a person didn't seem like a positive step forward.

'I don't think so. It'll be awkward enough without taking someone on a first date to witness my humiliation.' And she didn't know why she was beginning to talk as though she was actually going to acknowledge this engagement in person…

Undeterred, Ursula thrust her phone in front of Evie's face, forcing her to look at the list of dating sites and apps available. She was about to bat it away when something caught her eye.

'Fake date register… What's that?' she asked the expert.

Ursula frowned, tapping away at the screen. 'Exactly what it says. Apparently, you can "engage in a mutually beneficial arrangement with no strings or expectations". How boring.'

However, Evie's interest was piqued. 'So I could get someone to pretend to be my date, and all I'd have to do is be their "show girlfriend" in return? It might be a possibility.'

At least she wouldn't have to degrade herself by paying someone to do it. If she decided she was desperate enough to go down that route. It would certainly wipe the grins off some faces if she turned up at this engagement with a Bailey replacement, as though what had occurred was of no consequence to her whatsoever, and hadn't completely turned her world upside down.

She heard the familiar sound of a camera shutter as Ursula snapped a photograph.

'What are you doing?' a self-conscious Evie asked, aware that she wasn't wearing makeup, her hair had been tied up in a very messy bun and she was likely covered in clay as usual.

Ignoring her, Ursula continued tapping on her phone, the odd ping of notifications breaking her silence. Eventually she smiled and held up the screen for Evie to peer at.

'I've set up an account for you.'

'You've done what?' Evie grabbed the phone off her, staring in horror at the profile picture, every bit as hideous as she'd imagined. 'I look awful. Who the hell is going to want to date that mess? Besides which, I never agreed to anything. I was simply investigating the possibilities.'

Ursula pouted. 'I'm only trying to help. And you look adorable. There are several men who seem to agree.'

Before she could wrestle the phone back off Evie she saw for herself that there were some potential 'fake dates' in the mix. Perhaps this wasn't a completely off-the-wall idea after all.

'What do you mean, I'm unapproachable?' Jake barked at his sister, Donna, who also doubled up as his business partner. They ran Hanley Film Studios in Belfast's Titanic Quarter, which had become a thriving area for the television and film industry over the last fourteen years or so.

Although born in England, he'd completed his business degree in Belfast and, after a brief enterprise in London working in television, he'd made the move back to Northern Ireland to capitalise on the opportunities here. Donna had moved over to join him a year later, after her relationship ended and she needed a fresh start.

The petite blonde didn't look anything like him, and had a completely different disposition—one that had made her the friendly face of the company, rather than him. He didn't tend to make friends easily, and he didn't want to. Growing up as an army brat, he'd learned not to lean on anyone because they'd be out of his life soon enough.

Something he'd unfortunately carried over into his love life too. To the point he'd left the love of his life to focus on work. Now he was being told he should be 'nicer' to the people he paid.

'This,' she said, waving a hand in his general direction. 'You're spiky. And, if you haven't noticed, we have a high turnover of staff in the office. You're great at your job, but you're single-minded and it doesn't make for a great atmosphere. I'm telling you this for your own sake, to make life easier for you, and for everyone else here. Poor Patty is going to have a nervous breakdown if she has to come into your office to ask you for another training budget. Be kind.'

His mouth twitched into an almost smile. Timid Patty in Accounts was definitely not someone he wanted to lose, but it was true, she didn't stand up to him the way Donna did. He'd admit he wasn't always in the mood to discuss another ex-employee, or the fact that they needed to interview more potentials.

Jake relaxed his frown, took a deep breath and attempted a calm voice. 'What would you suggest?'

'It's coming up to Christmas. I know you don't like parties, but I do think you should attend something with your staff to get to know them better. So they can see that, behind the expensive tailored suits and perma-scowl, you are actually human. That those rumours you were created in a lab under a full moon aren't actually true.' Donna batted her impossibly long eyelashes and smiled a sickly-sweet smile.

Jake raised an eyebrow. She was dancing on thin ice here. Especially when she was sitting on his desk, on top of his paperwork, not showing an ounce of respect for anything. It was just as well she was important to him here as a liaison between him and the outside world or he might take exception to his little sister telling him what to do.

'Again, I ask: what would you suggest I do to make *friends* around here?'

There was a heavy dose of sarcasm in the request. He didn't need to make friends, but he could do with fewer interruptions in his working day. If it got Donna off his back, and his workforce could toil independently of his input, it might be worth a try.

'Well… I've heard about this place that does something called a pizza, prosecco and pottery night.'

'Sounds like my idea of hell,' he grumbled, imagining a room full of drunk women chucking clay around. He had no idea how that was going to improve working relations, and he wasn't about to reenact any romantic cinematic pottery scenes with his employees in order to gain some fans.

Donna slapped him not so playfully on the arm. 'It'll be fun. And I don't mean you pay for the evening and disappear. You'd have to stay and participate.' She whipped out a business card from her pocket and handed it to him. 'Here's the address.'

Clearly, she already had this planned out, and if he wanted rid of her so he could get on with his working day, he would have to at least make it seem as if there was a possibility of arranging this.

'Okay, okay, I'll think about it. Now, shoo. I have work to do.' He took the card and waved her out of his office.

Donna took her time getting up from his desk, brushed off her black and red body-con dress and narrowed her eyes at him. 'See? You need to be nicer to me. I'm not some household pest; I am an asset to you, Mr Grouchy-Pants. Without me, you'd just be some recluse all the local kids are scared of. I am the only thing standing between you and a midnight procession of villagers with torches at your door.'

With a swish of her hair, Donna left his office.

How could he argue with any of that?

It was late, as usual, when Jake finally left work. The place was dark and empty. Sometimes he preferred it that way. Just like the city streets at this time of night. At least when he went home at this time he missed the rush-hour traffic, and the ensuing madness of everyone trying to get home at the same time.

All he had to worry about here was driving on a dark, rainy December night.

As he waited at the traffic lights for the imaginary pedestrian who apparently needed to cross the road ahead of him, he happened to glance up at the building on the side of the road, an old converted mill now housing all manner of business units. He wondered why the street name seemed familiar, then he realised it was the address of the pottery place Donna had been so insistent about. On a whim, he clicked on his indicator and as soon as the green light flashed, he swerved onto the side road and into the car park in the grounds of the old mill buildings.

A quick glance around showed that many of the units were still open—a gym, a dance studio and oh, the pottery studio. A small sign attached to a heavy metal door proclaimed 'Evie Kerrigan's Ceramics Studio' was upstairs. He could see that the lights were still on and, after some hesitation, Jake decided to unbuckle his seatbelt and investigate the place for himself.

Upon hauling the heavy door open he was faced with a stone spiral staircase surrounded by whitewashed walls, a cold, unwelcoming entrance that spoke of the original building, but eventually gave way to a brightly lit corridor and more modern-looking facilities. He noted the business names on the doors until he came to the one he was looking for. With the door already open, he knocked and walked on in.

It took him a moment to see past the wooden workbenches and shelves laden with an assortment of wares, but eventually he focused his gaze on the figure at the right-hand side of the room. Head down, humming away to the songs on the radio, she clearly hadn't heard him enter the room. Jake took in the sight of her in her muddied apron and glasses while he waited.

Some snuffling at his feet alerted him to what seemed like a huge shaggy carpet laid before him. Then the creature raised its head and presented a half chewed, sodden teddy bear. Tail wagging with obvious excitement at sharing his prize with the stranger, he wasn't much of a guard dog.

'Dave! Come away! Sorry, I didn't hear you come in.'

'Dave?' Jake peered at the retriever type canine with amusement, ruffling his fur and setting the tail wagging at full speed again.

The bespectacled brunette wiped her hands

on an already dirty rag before getting to her feet to face him. 'Yes. He's my studio companion. It can get quite scary in here at night, and the place is rumoured to be haunted by a lady in white who apparently threw herself to her death from the top of the building. Mind you, I'm not sure Dave would do much to save me if I ever found myself in danger.'

'No, I don't think he'd be capable of scaring anyone away.'

Even Jake, who wasn't usually a fan of any four-legged friend, was becoming increasingly enamoured of the lumbering furry cutie who was now lying on his back expecting tummy rubs. More startling than that was the fact that Jake was kneeling on the dusty floor in his suit, obliging.

A pair of crusty old trainers began to move towards him.

'I thought you'd changed your mind about coming here tonight. If I'd known, I would've made myself more presentable. Although I know this isn't a date date.'

'Pardon me?' Jake stood up again in time to see the pretty potter shaking her long hair free from its elastic confines and wiping the clay from her glasses.

'I suppose you were a bit nervous, like me.

It's not the norm for either of us, I guess. Although, I have to say, you don't look gay. I mean, I know that's the wrong thing to say… not very PC, but I'm sure you could've found someone you know to do this for you.' The woman was rambling. He was frowning, and wondering why on earth she would've assumed he was gay.

'I'm sorry? It was my sister, Donna, who suggested this.'

'Oh. So you were talked into this too? I have a friend like that. What is it with the hideous profile pictures they insist on setting up? Yours doesn't look anything like you. You're more handsome than I thought. Although your fur baby was covering most of your face so it was hard to tell.' She rattled on nervously, making no sense whatsoever to Jake. His head was spinning, trying to make sense of what she was saying.

'I'm sorry, I have no idea what you're talking about. Thank you for the compliment, but the rest of that was lost on me. What's a fur baby? And where is it you think you've seen me before?'

Jake watched her cheeks pink. 'Your dog, Princess. She was in your profile picture.

That's what drew me to you on the Fake Date site.'

'Fake Date?'

Now her cheeks were scarlet as it began to dawn on her that he probably wasn't who she thought he was.

'The app. For matching people who need a pretend girlfriend/boyfriend for the night. You're not Olly Leadbetter, are you?'

'No, I'm Jake Hanley. Not on any dating sites that I know of. I don't have a dog called Princess, and I'm definitely not gay.'

But he was amused by the whole situation. There was something adorable about this woman, and it wasn't just the streaks of clay on her face and in her hair.

It was the fact that he was so at ease in the midst of her chaos.

Usually, he needed everything neat and orderly around him to feel comfortable, no doubt a throwback to his father's army-style parenting methods. It wasn't as though he wasn't used to highly strung women either. Patty from Accounts had her nails bitten down to the quick on a regular basis, and Donna only ever sat still if it was on top of his desk in the midst of his working day. But this was different. He was enjoying being in this woman's world, which seemed such a long way from his, and he was curious about what the hell was going on with her.

'Evie Kerrigan,' she said, then buried her face in her hands. 'I'm so sorry. I just assumed you were the guy I was supposed to meet tonight. Then he cancelled, and you showed up, and I just put two and two together.'

'And came up with a closeted gay dog owner?' He supposed it was an improvement on the village monster, and something which would make Donna cackle at the very thought.

'Ugh. Sorry. Again. Can we just forget about that? What can I do for you, Mr Hanley?'

'Jake. I actually came to see about arranging one of those pizza and pottery nights for my employees, but please, tell me more about this fake date thing, Evie.' He pulled over a high stool and sat down, waiting for her to spill the details.

Her laugh, a mixture of embarrassment and hilarity at her own faux pas, made him chuckle too, something he didn't do a lot of these days. Hell, he didn't even realise it was in his repertoire to do so.

'I can't. It's so unprofessional. And, may I say, uncharacteristic for me.' She bent down to cuddle the dog, buried her head in his fur, and eventually ended up lying on the floor with him.

He liked this crazy Evie woman.

'I haven't actually employed your services yet, and I do think you owe me some kind of explanation...'

Evie sighed and stretched flat out on the floor.

'My friend signed me up to this site so I can take a fake date home. Where my step-sister is getting engaged to my ex-boyfriend. That's sad, right?'

She rolled over onto her side and leaned on her elbow.

Jake considered the scenario, which seemed harsh for someone who appeared so nice. 'Practical, I'd say. Though I don't know why you'd want to be involved in that at all.'

'It's complicated. They're the only family I have, and I made a promise to my dad that I'd try and keep us together.'

'I'm sure he didn't mean for you to stick around to be walked over. These people screwed you over.' He was assuming she'd made the vow on her father's deathbed or something when she seemed so tied into the idea.

Evie winced and flopped back over onto

her back, with a concerned Dave lying beside her. 'I know, I know. For the past fifteen years I've been treated as though I'm nothing more than a nuisance. Ursula thinks I need closure. They broke my heart, but I picked myself up and started my own business. I shouldn't be lying here thinking I'm a failure because the people I loved most in the world broke my trust. And why is this beginning to feel like a therapy session?'

'Should I get my notebook and pen?'

'I'm sorry. None of this has anything to do with you. You only came in to book a session. Which I'm going to have to heavily discount now if there's any hope of you coming back. I swear I'm not usually this much of a mess.' Evie got back onto her feet with another sigh, which seemed to come from the depths of her very soul.

'So this is about revenge?'

'More a case of not wanting to humiliate myself further. Although asking a stranger to pretend to be my boyfriend isn't exactly the dream scenario.'

'Sounds practical to me.'

Evie cocked her head to one side. 'You don't think I'm crazy?'

'I never said that.' He grinned. There weren't

many strangers who were willing to even approach him, never mind share such a personal story on a first meet. He supposed it was only because of a case of mistaken identity, but he got the impression from this brief interaction that Evie Kerrigan wore her heart on her sleeve. Something which, in the circumstances, was probably going to set her up for another fall with these horrid people in her life.

At least he'd managed to make her smile.

'Well, thank you. I think.'

'Honestly, I think it's a good idea. I have a…thing to go to. It would be easier if I had someone to accompany me. No strings, no complications or expectations.' The cogs were beginning to whirr now with the possibilities of this kind of arrangement.

Evie's eyes were as wide as saucers. 'Wait. Are you actually considering doing this with me?'

'Yes, I am. My mother's getting remarried and I'll be expected to take a plus one. I don't want the hassle of asking someone who'll read more into it.'

Plus, Evie was sweet and amiable. She could probably act as a barrier between him and a legion of people he didn't really want to talk to. Including his parents.

'Okay…but I don't know anything about you. At least with Olly I had an idea of the person I was going to be taking home with me.'

Despite being the answer to her prayers, she was now eyeing him suspiciously, her arms folded defensively across her chest, as though he often spent his nights trawling old buildings in search of women going through an emotional crisis.

Honestly, he was offended.

'My name is Jake Hanley. I'm thirty-four, an army brat who moved from country to country with his parents, and who now also runs his own business and is too busy for "normal" relationships. I only came here because my sister, Donna, suggested I needed to bond with my workforce. Apparently, I'm too…unapproachable. Something about villagers chasing me with torches and pitchforks if I don't make an effort.' He wasn't sure any of that information would help her to believe he wasn't a danger, but it was the truth.

It had been a day for uncomfortable truths.

Evie was smirking by the end of his introduction. Arms unfolded. Ice broken.

'Okay, I believe you, and I can see we both need each other. We will also have to get our stories straight if we're ever going to convince anyone that we're a couple. But it's getting late. Why don't we meet up to discuss the details some other time?'

'It's a date.' He couldn't resist getting one last rise out of her before walking away, her side-eye putting a little pep in his step.

Today had been full of surprises, but the biggest one had been meeting someone who took his mind off everything except her.

Donna would be impressed. Exactly why he wasn't going to tell her anything about Evie Kerrigan.

CHAPTER TWO

'YOU DO GET yourself into some terrible messes, Evie Kerrigan.' She took a sip of her luxury hot chocolate, keeping her eye on the door of the coffee shop for her 'date'.

Fake date, she reminded herself. Though she still couldn't figure out exactly how this had happened. One minute she was happily working in her studio, the next she was lying on the floor spilling her guts out to a complete stranger. Who, by all accounts, had serious issues of his own. And she'd just agreed to take him home with her in an attempt to convince the people who'd broken her heart that she was happy.

This didn't have disaster written all over it at all!

She was on the verge of texting Jake back to say perhaps this wasn't a good idea when he swept into the coffee shop. He looked completely out of place among the groups of chatting mothers, phone obsessed teens and crossword-filling pensioners. With his slicked-back hair, long wool coat and his handsome dark looks, he looked as though he'd just stepped out of an aftershave advert.

Even her heart gave a little gasp at the sight of him, and she knew why he was here. To concoct a fake relationship because he was too busy to entertain the idea of a real one. Not exactly the stuff dreams were made of, but what she needed right now.

'Jake!' She raised a hand to get his attention, then quickly dropped it as every pair of eyes in the place suddenly swivelled towards her, as if to ask why on earth this perfect specimen of masculinity was here to see *her*.

He strode over towards her table. 'I need coffee.' Then did an about-turn towards the counter.

Evie gulped her chocolate, wishing for something more than cream and marshmallows to steel her for this encounter. He looked even more handsome and out of her league in daylight and she wondered how the hell they were going to fool anyone into thinking they were a couple.

It wasn't long before he was back, clutching a small cup of espresso. 'Thanks for coming on such short notice, but I'm a busy man. As I'm sure you're a busy woman.'

Evie nodded, though she was sure throwing cups and vases wasn't as draining as whatever he did for a job. At least she got to sit down, listen to the radio and drink as many cups of tea as she could manage. She could picture him shouting into a phone at the stock market, or something equally stressful.

'I wasn't expecting to hear from you so soon, but I suppose we have a lot to sort out.' Despite their agreement last night, his text this morning had come as something of a surprise. Needless to say, she'd spent the couple of hours since brushing her hair, putting on some make-up and making herself presentable.

'Yes. In all the excitement, I forgot to ask when this engagement party was.'

'Saturday.'

He almost spat his coffee in her face. 'So soon?'

'Yes. Sorry. I completely understand if you can't make it.'

'No. We made a deal. I'll just swap a few things around in my schedule.' He took out his phone and started tapping, making her feel special that he was even giving her the time of day, never mind committing to a whole evening with her family.

'Hopefully, we won't have to stay too long. Just dinner and a couple of drinks to toast the happy couple.' She tried and failed to keep the sarcasm and bitterness from her voice. Only time would tell if she'd be able to overcome that over the course of the following few days.

'Where is it?'

'Bangor. County Down,' she said, for reference. The supposed moneyed part of the country. Yet where she'd grown up virtually having to fend for herself financially once her father died. It was funny that her stepsister had never been expected to get a menial part-time job, unlike Evie, who'd worked in retail and hospitality to fund her time at university. Yet even now she didn't know how Courtney earned the money to keep her in the lifestyle to which she'd become accustomed. No doubt banker Bailey had a lot to do with that.

'I'll drive. What time?'

'I haven't told them I'm coming yet.'

Jake glanced up from his screen to give her a look of disapproval.

'I'll confirm tonight. It'll probably be about six-ish, and home no later than ten, I imagine.'

'I'll need your address to pick you up. Which I assume will be around five o'clock.'

She nodded, feeling slightly as though she was being interviewed in a speed date fashion, where every second and word counted. He wasn't wasting either on small talk, and she was beginning to see why his sister had pushed him into being more sociable. This work version of Mr Hanley wasn't smiling and teasing like out of hours Jake who'd turned up unexpectedly in her studio last night. Though she supposed that was a good thing for her personally, so she wouldn't be blinded by good looks, and potentially hitch her wagon to yet another wrong horse.

'In terms of our story…where should we say we met?'

She needed something plausible and it was going to be obvious to everyone that they didn't move in the same social circles. He looked like someone who'd just walked out of a catalogue, and she looked like someone who simply stroked the pages lovingly, wishing she could afford the contents.

Though in this instance no money had changed hands. He wasn't an escort and she wasn't desperate, or rich, enough to pay for his services. She was sure Jake Hanley would be an expensive investment, though probably worth it…

When she realised the full lips she was staring at were moving, those cool blue eyes staring at her, she had to refocus.

'Sorry. I didn't catch that.'

He huffed out an exasperated breath. 'I said we should stick as close to the truth as possible so we don't trip up.'

'You mean tell them you came to book a class and I mistook you for my gay fake date, before launching into details of my romantic trauma?'

'Hmm, we can probably skip that part. We'll just say I stopped by to book a class and things went from there. It's early days though, so that should cover us for not knowing everything there is to know about each other.'

'Good idea. Courtney and Bailey would laugh themselves into a coma if they knew the truth.'

'And that would be bad because…?' The twinkle was back in his eyes that she'd seen last night.

Evie preferred this warm, funny Jake, as opposed to the efficient, no-nonsense Mr Hanley who'd first come through the door. She was all about the nonsense.

'Because I don't want them to know they hurt me so badly I don't even want to risk being with anyone else.'

She didn't want to bring the tone back down again but she wanted to be honest with him. Ironic, in the circumstances. But it was important he knew how big of a deal it was going to be for her to face Courtney and Bailey again.

'I get that.' He nodded, but what else could he say to that other than telling her to man up and forget about them? Ursula had tried the tough love approach with her and it hadn't worked so far.

'So, tell me about your event. What do I need to know?'

He sat back in his chair, looking uncomfortable before he'd even opened his mouth. Evie was glad this was a two-way deal so she wouldn't feel vulnerable on her own, opening up like this with someone she hardly knew. Clearly, Jake had his personal problems with his family too.

'Mum's getting married soon to someone I hardly know. She moved over here after Donna and I did, and met Gary. He's one in a long line of boyfriends since she and my dad divorced. They're still friends, so he'll be there too. I'd rather not be. They're not the advert for good parents, or relationships, but I don't want to cause a drama. I just need a buffer. That's where you come in.'

So now the price she was going to have to pay for his assistance was becoming clear. If his family were half as scary as he had a tendency to be, Evie wasn't sure she'd be the partner he needed for the occasion.

'Your dad's ex-army, right?'

'Yes, but don't worry, he probably won't stick around long. He never did.'

There was a poignancy to his words that made her think he wasn't as indifferent to his parents as he was making out. He'd clearly been hurt too.

'Is this going to be a fancy "do"? Will it require me wearing something not covered in clay?' Clearly, she was going to have to get a new outfit but she wasn't sure what level of couture would be required, and if she needed to remortgage her flat so she could afford something suitable.

'I imagine so, but I'll cover any expenses.' He whipped out a credit card and slid it across the table.

'You trust me, a stranger, with your credit card?' She could do some serious damage with that if left unsupervised. Like pay off all her bills and buy a new spray gun for her glazes.

'Well, there's a chance you could empty my bank account and flee the country, but I get the impression you want to see this engagement party through. And you seem to like your work so…'

'Right on both counts. Where do you want to go?' She didn't imagine he did much shopping in the charity shops or discount stores she usually frequented. There wasn't much point in wearing expensive clothes in her line of work when they ended up covered in clay and glaze. She dressed for comfort, and warmth, to limit the possibility of freezing to death in that draughty old building.

Jake frowned. 'I'm not going dress shopping with you. That's why I'm giving you the card. I don't really even have time to be here.'

'Of course. It's just… I'm not sure what's appropriate. It's okay. I'm sure I'll figure it out.' What was she expecting? That he was going to do a Richard Gere and take her shopping on Rodeo Drive? This wasn't some romantic fantasy; it was an attempt to survive her heartbreak.

'I'm sure you'll be fine. You look lovely

today. Better. Than last night,' he stuttered, showing that even the seemingly unflappable Jake could get flustered.

Evie didn't know which one of them was blushing more at the unintended compliment. Yes, she was ignoring the follow-on comment because he'd said she looked lovely. It wasn't an everyday occurrence for her to hear that. Not only because she didn't dress to impress on a daily basis, but because usually the only people she ever saw in her studio were Ursula, customers and, of course, Dave.

Then again, she'd actually made an effort today, knowing she was seeing Jake. She'd wanted to look nice for him, and to feel good about herself after making such a crazy first impression on him. So she'd donned her prettiest winter dress, emblazoned with holly berries, tied neatly at her waist, and teamed with a dark green cardigan. There was no way she was letting him take that back. Not now, when her heart was beginning to flutter. A miracle when she was sure Bailey's antics had all but killed it.

'I'll ask Ursula for advice. She goes to enough of these things to know what I should wear.'

Other than not turning up in white, Evie

didn't know a lot about wedding attire etiquette, or high society functions. Her studio assistant, on the other hand, seemed to live her life in a whirlwind of parties and socialising. Probably why she'd hired her. Ursula was better at the people side of the business. When she thought about it, Jake would probably have been better off taking Ursula to this thing. Although she didn't want to lose him when she was just getting used to the idea that she was going to have someone to support her through this difficult time.

Jake's ringing phone prevented him from having to concern himself with the small matter of her wardrobe. He tossed back his coffee and got up from his seat. 'Great. I'll see you on Saturday and we'll talk about it then.'

Focused now on whoever was calling, he disappeared out of the door, clearly a busy man. Evie considered herself lucky he'd spared her these few minutes of his precious time. He must've really wanted backup for this wedding when he'd agreed to grant her an entire Saturday evening.

Now Evie had more to worry about than showing herself up in front of just her ex and her stepfamily.

The screen flashed on her phone with an incoming call.

'Speak of the devil,' she muttered, seeing her stepmother's name.

For a moment she considered not answering, but she knew she'd have to face up to the inevitable. Especially now that Jake was rearranging his busy schedule to accompany her to the event of the year.

'Hey, June.' She'd never been able to bring herself to call her 'Mum'. That role had been taken long ago, even if Evie didn't remember her mother, who'd died of peritonitis when she was little more than a baby. Not that June would've wanted that anyway.

She hadn't been the maternal figure for Evie her dad had probably hoped she'd be after raising his daughter alone until her teenage years. In contrast to her own daughter, whom she'd showered with praise and money, June had treated Evie like a lodger at best. At worst, a skivvy around the house, doing the chores neither she nor Courtney were prepared to do, as if Evie had a duty to earn her keep in the house she'd grown up in long before they'd come on the scene. It had always been just Evie and her father for as long as she could remember. Her mother was nothing more than some faded photographs. And even they'd been hidden away once June arrived.

Still, they were her only family, and they did still include her in these get-togethers. Even if she didn't always want to be there.

'We haven't heard from you about your sister's engagement. You are coming, aren't you? I know there was some unpleasantness some time ago, but that's all past us now.'

Speak for yourself.

'Yes. I'm coming.'

'Alone?' It was such a loaded word. A question not only about her relationship status but also her mental state. Was she going to cause a scene with her bitterness, or just celebrate with the happy couple?

Neither, but at least she'd have Jake there in her corner.

'No. I'm bringing someone with me.'

'Oh, good. I just want you to be happy for your sister.'

Evie was twitching at the fact she was still being painted as the one in the wrong. Though that was always going to be the way between the two of them where her stepmother was concerned. Her precious little Courtney could never do any wrong. Even if she had slept with her stepsister's boyfriend behind her back.

'I'll be there.' That was as much as she could promise.

'And who's this young man you're bringing? Tell me all about him. Courtney will want to know the details.'

Eve's stomach somersaulted at the mere mention of her date. Goodness knew how she was going to get through a whole night with him in their company without breaking cover. The idea of Courtney analysing their every move made her want to throw up. Evie was neither a good liar nor a great actress. Two things her stepsister apparently excelled at. Ironically, she might be able to spot the fake.

'His name's Jake. We're not long together, so take it easy on him.'

She tried to make light of it, though she knew there was no chance they weren't going to sit through an interrogation about their 're-lationship'. She only hoped she could withstand the intense questioning. As for Jake, she wasn't sure which side of him would be better suited to this meet-the-family scenario. Though she preferred the Jake who'd turned up at her studio last night, and he would certainly charm everyone, today's cool customer might be more to her advantage. He wouldn't give anything away, and probably make everyone else feel insignificant and inferior. Yet she would feel more comfortable with the relaxed Jake who'd actually seemed interested in her problems. The man she could actually see herself being with.

'Is he handsome?'

'Yes.' The answer to that one came easily.

Trust June to be so shallow when it came to a suitable partner. The next thing she'd be asking would be about his annual income. Evie wouldn't put it past her if she tried to matchmake with Courtney if she knew the truth. Jake was a much better prospect than cheating Bailey.

'Ooh. Can't wait to meet him.'

'Well, I have to get back to work, but we'll see you on Saturday.'

'Oh, yes, I'm sure those teacups won't make themselves.' The sneering was there as always when it came to talk of Evie's career.

It didn't matter that she had a degree and ran her own business, as far as her family was concerned, she just played with clay for a living. Which to some extent was true, but she also thought she deserved some level of respect for making a success of it.

Evie hung up before June could ask any more questions about Jake which she probably wouldn't be able to answer, or insult her any further, feeling as though she'd mentally just gone ten rounds in a boxing ring.

It occurred to her that their getting-to-know-one-another meeting at the coffee shop this morning hadn't achieved much other than the confirmation that he hadn't changed his mind about the whole thing. She didn't know any more about him. Not enough to withstand any intensive questioning. They were going to have to wing it. It wasn't exactly the ideal plan when trying to convince her family she was in a committed, loving relationship. Only time would tell if it was inviting more pain and humiliation into her life, but at this point she didn't have anything left to lose.

CHAPTER THREE

'I CAN ONLY apologise in advance for anything anyone does or says.' Evie was getting in early, absolving herself of any responsibility, as they drove to her family home.

Jake smiled. 'It's fine. I have a good idea of what I'm getting myself into.'

'You have no idea…'

'Families are all a nightmare. You'll be returning the favour soon enough.'

It was another hint that he had some deep-seated issues with his parents which didn't sound as though they'd be resolved any time soon.

She couldn't help but push a little on the matter so he'd remember the reason they both needed this to work.

'Is your mother a shallow, passive-aggressive nightmare too?' she asked, batting the false eyelashes she was worried weren't going to survive the night before she ripped them off.

'Worse.' Jack pursed his lips together. 'She's a romantic.'

The unexpected horror on his face at the revelation made her laugh hard. 'How terrible for you.'

Jake took his eyes off the road for a moment to narrow them at her. 'You have no idea. She falls in love every five minutes. Only this time she's apparently making it to the altar. I have no idea how she and my father ever thought it would work between them when he's so…grounded.'

'Maybe she's just an optimist.' It didn't sound so bad having a mother who apparently saw possibilities in everyone. A definite contrast to her family, who thought she was a lost cause.

'She's that all right. I seem to spend my whole life defending my decision to focus on work instead of "settling down". Be prepared for a barrage of questions about when we're having babies when it's time for you to return the favour.'

It took a moment for her to remember to laugh at the absurdity of that when her mind had taken her somewhere unexpected and erotic. A wistful wondering about what her and Jake's babies would look like had quickly taken her to the conception. Her imagination was conjuring up pictures of him in a state of undress, what was hidden behind the designer suits and the very efficient exterior. Meanwhile, her body was already reacting to the idea of what he would be like in the bedroom. Warm and engaging, or efficient, wasting no time in getting to a successful conclusion? Either way, her interest was piqued way beyond someone she was only with to convince her family she was over their betrayal. Perhaps she was finally getting over it, and some day she might be able to get back on the dating scene for real. This was certainly the first time since Bailey she'd felt anything like this for another man. Probably only because this was the closest she'd ever let herself get to one, through fear for what was left of her self-esteem as well as her heart.

Evie shifted uncomfortably in her seat, the confines of his car, where she could feel his body heat, and smell his intoxicating cologne, suddenly becoming stifling.

'Can we turn the radio on?'

She fiddled with the console before he'd even had time to give an answer, needing a distraction, something to create the illusion of distance between them at least, the only consolation being that they were almost at their destination. It said a lot about her current state of mind when she was thinking of her family as the lesser of two evils, ready to face their certain disapproval and disregard over whatever she was beginning to feel for Jake. A man she didn't know, and wasn't supposed to actually be involved with beyond this deception.

'There is a weather warning across the province, with snow showers predicted later this evening.'

The weather forecast on the radio didn't do anything to ease the tightness in her chest.

'Should we be worried, do you think?' It was one thing feeling as though she should put in an appearance as a show of good will, but quite another if they were endangering their lives to get there and back.

'I checked the forecast before we left and it looks as though the worst of the snow will hit the area overnight, so we should be okay if we only spend a couple of hours. The motorways and main roads will be gritted anyway. I'm sure we'll get back.' Jake's confidence was reassuring, because she knew there was no way he'd risk taking extra time out of his life for such a non-event.

'It'll be a good excuse to leave early, at least. Dinner, drinks, and out of there as soon as possible.' That was the plan and if they stuck to it, hopefully, there wouldn't be time for them to be rumbled, or for Evie to suffer too many barbed comments.

'I won't be drinking. Driving, remember?'

'I wasn't talking about you,' she muttered. Not usually a big drinker, she knew she'd need some Dutch courage to get through this. Or at least a few glasses of wine.

'No being sick in the car. That's my number one rule.'

'Yes, sir.' She saluted him, but understood why he wouldn't want the pristine interior of his sleek ride sullied by her inability to function normally around her family.

'Stop worrying. I'm here for you, okay?' He pulled on the handbrake as they arrived outside their destination and turned to her, his intense blue eyes filled with a genuine concern for her that she wasn't used to.

She bit her lip as she nodded, trying not to burst into tears and make a fool of herself before they'd even set foot inside the house.

'Let's do this.' She took a deep breath and got ready to face the firing squad, all the while wondering why she felt like she was the one who'd done something wrong when all she was guilty of was being too trusting. And, after today, of faking her happiness with a new partner. It wasn't as though she'd got caught in bed with her stepsister's boyfriend and gone on to become his fiancée.

The anxiety must've been coming off her in waves as they crunched across the gravel driveway in the dark as Jake reached out and took her hand, giving it a squeeze as she rang the doorbell and offering her a smile as they awaited admittance. Enough to remind her she had his support, and he actually cared about how she was feeling. Enough for her poor wounded heart to give one last gasp before it threw in the towel altogether. Perhaps she wasn't completely done with men altogether if there were still nice ones like Jake Hanley out there, capable of making her feel safe, even for a couple of hours.

Her pulse picked up an extra beat with the sound of every stiletto step towards the front door.

'Evelyn!'

'Evie,' she mumbled as her stepmother gripped her by the shoulders and delivered two air kisses.

'And this must be your beau.'

Evie cringed as Jake was swamped by June's enhanced cleavage in a more demonstrative hug than she'd ever received.

'Jake,' she corrected.

'You must come and meet everyone, Jakie.' June grabbed for his hand, forcing Evie and Jake apart.

Even though he wasn't actually hers, Evie felt the loss immediately. He managed to flash her an apologetic look before he was dragged further into the house in front of her. She was left to close the door as he was spirited away to be introduced to the awaiting crowd, whilst she was an afterthought. As usual.

Evie hung up her coat and bag, checked her reflection in the full-size hall mirror and took a deep breath before entering the fray.

The lounge was packed with people, and the room full of chat and laughter, a full assault on the senses when combined with the smell of food and expensive perfumes. Not to mention the mouthful of wine from the glass she helped herself to from the buffet table set up at the far side of the room.

'Mummy thought we should celebrate at the golf club, but we thought we should keep things low-key. Intimate. It didn't seem right to have a huge party.' Courtney was nursing a glass of her own as she approached Evie, insincerity oozing from every make-up camouflaged pore.

'How considerate.' More likely they couldn't afford to put it on at the exclusive venue, or Bailey had put his foot down. He wasn't one for splashing his cash around, which made their match even more baffling. One thing was certain, they weren't doing any of this for Evie's benefit.

Courtney was dressed in a gold and champagne lace mini dress, her honey-coloured hair swept up at the sides and secured with a diamond barrette, leaving soft romantic waves falling to her shoulders. She looked sufficiently beautiful, and expensive, to make Evie feel inadequate. When Evie had put on her wine-red velvet wrap-over dress and done her make-up and hair, she'd been pleased with her reflection, along with the appreciative look Jake had afforded her at the door. Now, however, she was reminded why she hadn't been enough for Bailey. At least by bringing a fake date she didn't have to worry that history might repeat itself.

'Thanks for coming, Evester. We appreciate it.' Bailey's obnoxious nickname was equally as aggravating as June's insistence on using her full name.

'Bailey.' She couldn't bring herself to do anything other than acknowledge his presence. Though in her head she was chucking her drink in his face and mashing some of that fancy salmon mousse in his face.

'Honestly, we didn't think you'd show your face here again after all the histrionics.'

A smug Bailey slid his arm around Courtney's teeny-tiny waist as though he was claiming his prize, leaving Evie feeling as though she was the loser in all of this. It was mind-boggling to her now what she'd ever seen in him, or why she'd been so bothered about them being together in the first place, other than their sneaking around behind her back. They were welcome to each other.

Evie considered going home now that she'd apparently made peace with the situation and done her duty by giving them her blessing, when she felt a pair of strong arms wrapping around her.

'Sorry, babe. June wanted to show me around. I missed you.' Jake hugged her close against his hard body, his face pressed against hers so she could feel the rasp of his stubble on her face and his hot breath in her ear.

She almost let out a squeal, giving the game away, then she remembered they were supposed to be a couple and this level of intimacy should be the norm. Doing her best to relax into the embrace, she leaned back and stroked the side of his face.

The flare of Bailey's nostrils and clenched jaw only made her want to act up more.

'I missed you too, sweetie. I was just telling Courtney they shouldn't have downsized their celebration on my account. We're all good.' Bolstered by scoring a point over them, she spun around and planted a kiss on Jake's lips.

The gruesome twosome soon lost interest and wandered back to the rest of their guests, leaving Evie to deal with the consequences of her actions.

Her face was flushed, and not just from the wine. Jake still had his arms around her, their bodies packed tightly together, and she could still feel the impression of his surprisingly soft lips on hers.

'Sorry,' she whispered, aware that kissing her hadn't been in the brief, but she'd taken his cue and run with it. All the way out of both of their comfort zones.

'It's okay. I think we did a good job of convincing them.' He sounded as breathless as she felt.

'Ladies and gentlemen, can I have your attention, please?' Her stepmother called everyone together and once Evie and Jake realised they were still clinging on to one another they sprang apart.

The general hubbub subsided until Evie was sure the only sound that could be heard was her heart, jolted back to life with the electricity from spontaneously kissing her unsuspecting date.

'I just want to thank everyone for coming to celebrate my beautiful daughter's engagement to my favourite future son-in-law, Bailey.' June raised a glass to the couple basking in glory in the centre of the room.

There was that vomit feeling coming that had Jake so concerned about the integrity of his upholstery.

Evie half-heartedly clapped along with everyone else so her urge to barf wasn't blatantly obvious.

'It hasn't been an easy time since I lost Len, but I know he'd be proud of his daughter. I just wish he could be here to walk you down the aisle. He was the only father you ever truly had, and I know you were the daughter he always wanted, Courtney.'

Another round of applause, but Evie couldn't join in this time as her hands were now clenched into fists.

'Just breathe.' Jake leaned in and though his close proximity didn't do anything to ease the tension in her body, it did manage to divert her attention away from the verbal assault going on.

Evie was the one he would be proud of, because she'd made something of her life, and had done it without any help, or managing to hurt anyone. Apart from anything else, *she* was his daughter. That wasn't something else June and Courtney could just take away from her because they felt like it. It wasn't her fault that Courtney's real father had never wanted anything to do with her, and it didn't mean they could just steal hers. Yes, he'd loved Courtney, but he would not have been happy to see them try and erase Evie from history. The only saving grace was that he wasn't here, and she wouldn't have to suffer further indignity watching him walk Courtney down the aisle to marry *her* ex-boyfriend.

On Jake's advice, she took deep breaths

and waited for the rage to subside. Only for Courtney to take centre stage.

'Thanks, Mum. I'm so grateful to have you and Bailey in my life, and lucky that we're going to be one big happy family soon.'

'Honestly, it's like I don't even exist sometimes,' Evie muttered under her breath.

Jake reached for another glass of wine and handed it to her, adding fuel to her fire.

'Like every couple, we've had our ups and downs. And kissed our fair share of frogs along the way.'

Jake's hand was on her arm now, as though he was ready to restrain her should she suddenly lunge at the blushing bride-to-be.

'But we've finally found each other.'

Ha! Evie had found him first, and Courtney and Bailey had known each other for quite some time before they'd decided to betray her.

'And I'm so lucky you took a chance on me.' Now it was Bailey's turn to increase the ick factor. 'My life had no meaning before you were part of it.'

'I've heard enough,' Evie fumed quietly to Jake, setting down her drink and making a sharp exit from the room.

It was one thing making an appearance, and getting some closure, but something different listening to her only meaningful relationship be dismissed so casually. As though she, and it, had meant nothing, when the brutal end of it had caused her so much heartache. Clearly, these two had no crisis of conscience about what they'd done to her, but she didn't have to stick around to hear them rub her nose in it. It wasn't jealousy fuelling her ire, but the injustice. They'd hurt her, betrayed her trust, and irrevocably changed her life. Yet neither of them seemed to care what they'd done to her. As always, her feelings were irrelevant here, and she'd been brutally reminded of that.

What made it worse was that it was happening in front of Jake in real time, opening his eyes to the loser she was, and likely always would be, at least in the eyes of her family. If she'd harboured any notion that he would come to like her in any romantic fashion, this debacle had poured cold water all over that. Everything about this party said that she could never be enough for anyone.

Evie fled the room before the tears fell, or she actually did punch someone and irreconcilably damaged the relationship she did have with her family. Bailey was going to marry Courtney and be a part of her life and she was going to have to get used to that. For now, though, she needed a little breathing space, and sought solace in her old bedroom.

Surprisingly, June hadn't altered it at all. Probably because the boxroom wasn't considered grand enough to use for anything other than an unwanted stepdaughter. However, right now, it was a familiar sanctuary for Evie to hide away for a while. The boy band posters on the wall and sketches she'd done herself pinned to her noticeboard spoke of the naïve teen she'd once been. Although the celestial themed navy and gold bedcovers had some other more unpleasant memories of the naïve adult she'd remained until her heart had been spectacularly demolished.

Her attempt to slam the door shut like all overemotional teens was halted by a shiny leather loafer as Jake stepped into the room behind her.

'Are you okay?' he asked, handing her a handkerchief. She hadn't even known that men still carried those—something she'd thought dreamed up solely for handsome men to dish out to distressed heroines in period dramas.

'I'm fine,' she insisted, then blew her nose noisily on the white cotton.

'They're idiots. You know that?' Jake looked

ridiculous perched on the end of her bed, too big to fit comfortably in here.

'Then why am I letting them get to me?' She threw herself dramatically onto the mattress beside him.

'Because you're normal. You have feelings and emotions, which these people don't seem to possess. Sorry, I know they're your family.'

'You know this is where I caught them? On my bed. As though they wanted me to find them. Courtney has her own princess bed in a room twice the size of this one, but no, they decided to have sex in my bed, and act shocked when I walked in.' The image was burned onto her eyeballs for ever, indelible scars left on her heart.

'There are people in this world who get off on inflicting pain on others. It's not a reflection on you, it's on them.'

'I think Courtney wanted to prove she could take him from me. To prove he didn't love me any more than she or June did.'

'As I said, they're both idiots, and you're better off without them.'

'So why can't I get over it?'

'You will. It's hard when you think you're going to spend the rest of your life with someone, only to realise you're better off on your own.' He kicked off his shoes and stretched out flat until his head was lying on the pillow beside her and his feet were hanging over the edge of the mattress.

'There speaks a man of experience.' She couldn't imagine anyone cheating on Jake, and thinking there was a better alternative, when he seemed like the complete package to her. Good looks, financial stability and compassionate—a woman would be lucky to have him as a life partner.

He sighed. 'I was with someone for a long time. Lacey. We lived in England together.'

'What happened?'

'Me. Work. You have to remember I spent my whole life moving from country to country with my parents. At least until my mother got sick of it, and decided my father wasn't the romantic hero she'd imagined, never around for any of us. Anyway, I met Lacey when I lived in London with my mum, and eventually we moved in together. We both worked at the TV studios there, but I wanted to go into business myself. I saw the opportunities here when big movie companies started to come here for filming. I realised there was a need for studios and wanted to buy some land to build my own. It was a huge opportunity and I had to take some big risks with investors but I knew it would be worth it. It made sense to move here, and since I'd gone to university in Belfast, I knew the city well. I had faith that I could really make something of myself here.'

'And she didn't want to come with you?'

He shook his head. 'She wanted to stay in London and raise a family, and that wasn't something I was ready to commit to. I didn't want to let that kind of business opportunity slip through my fingers on the basis that we might be the one couple who'd live happily ever after. Life's not like that. Mine certainly isn't.'

'Do you regret it?' Perhaps Jake wasn't the perfect man she'd imagined if he couldn't even commit to someone who'd obviously loved him.

'Honestly? No. I think it proves we weren't meant to be. I'm happy with my life, and I think she did get married and have the babies she wanted in England. My point is, you don't have to stay in a relationship that clearly isn't right just for the sake of it. Sometimes you're better off on your own, and as far as I can see you're doing all right. Much better than any of these morons are giving you credit for.'

He seemed to have the knack for making her smile even when she was at her lowest.

'You don't think you'll ever settle down with anyone?'

It was a depressing thought to imagine herself alone for ever, but these feelings Jake had seemed to awaken in her gave her an inkling that she hadn't completely given up on the idea of love and being with someone. She just had to make sure it was the right person. Someone who loved her as much as she loved them, and wouldn't jump into bed with her stepsister the second her back was turned.

'Never say never, but I've learned not to get close to anyone because you'll inevitably end up on your own anyway. What about you? Has this put you off relationships for life?'

'I hope not. I'd like to have someone other than Dave to cuddle in bed.'

'You don't need a loser like Bailey in your life for that. Come here.'

She scooched over and Jake put an arm around her, gathering her close. Head leaning on his chest, she listened to the steady, reassuring sound of his heart beating and the tension began to leave her body.

'What do you want to do now?' he asked, and she had to tell herself he was talking about the situation beyond this room, not what usually happened when two adults got into bed together.

'Can we just stay here for a while? Until everyone else has gone home?'

'Sure.'

Evie snuggled into him and closed her eyes, enjoying this sensation of safety in his arms. When she was here, Courtney and Bailey didn't even enter her head.

CHAPTER FOUR

IT WAS PITCH-BLACK when Jake opened his eyes and it took a few seconds for him to remember where he was. At the same moment he realised he was spooning Evie, and his body apparently didn't know this wasn't the time to react to being pressed tightly against a beautiful woman's behind. He moved away to compose himself, but Evie's little moan as he did so didn't help his painful predicament.

He stared at the ceiling, at the sparse bare bulb hanging there, wishing away what a lot of men would pay good money over the chemist's counter to have.

Evie was upset and vulnerable, and his arousal was inappropriate on so many levels. The least of which being that they weren't even on a real date. However, the more time he spent around her, the more he liked her, and the more he felt as though he should protect her. Especially from those she considered family but who, as far as he was concerned, were toxic.

As they'd belittled her, and her achievements, in front of friends and family, it had taken a great deal of control not to come out swinging, or sweep her up into his arms and carry her away from it all. He supposed he had one thing to thank his father for. The disciplinarian had instilled in him the importance of self-control when it came to emotions. Whilst it hadn't been all that useful in terms of relationships, at least it prevented situations like this from escalating.

It hadn't been beyond him to provide Evie with some comfort though, and she'd obviously needed it. He'd surprised himself, not only by offering it, but in how much he'd enjoyed simply cuddling her on the bed. Due to their arrangement, he didn't have to worry about what happened next or either of them getting too attached when this was a temporary setup. So he'd been able to reap the benefits of holding her close without having to deal with any of the potential complications. He had to admit it was nice to wake up with a woman in his arms again, someone he knew more about than simply a first name. On the occasions he had shared a bed with anyone since moving to Belfast, he'd been sure to keep things casual and uncomplicated, which had suited him until now. He simply had to remember that this was where it stopped with Evie, because she was the sort of woman who needed, and deserved, more than she'd been afforded in her relationships to date. Despite their similarities, he wasn't the man to give her that. Relationships simply weren't for him. No matter how attractive a prospect Evie was to him right now.

'What time is it?' she mumbled in the darkness.

Jake grabbed his phone and the screen lit up the room. 'It's eight o'clock.'

Evie scrambled to sit up. 'What? How did that happen?'

'We must have both fallen asleep.'

He went over to the window and opened the curtains, his heart sinking when he saw the thick blanket of snow sparkling in the moonlight. His was the only car still parked out front, almost completely covered in the white stuff.

Evie appeared beside him. 'Oh, no. How are we going to get out of here?'

'Maybe your stepmother has a shovel in the garage. Everyone else seems to have managed to get out.' Though any tyre tracks away from the property had been long since hidden with another layer of snow.

They made their way downstairs and into the lounge, where June, Courtney and Bailey were cleaning up the remnants of the party.

'Oh, you've decided to show your face again, then?' Courtney sniffed.

'Why didn't anyone wake us?'

It was the first time he'd seen Evie look angry. He guessed she really wanted to get away from here, and he couldn't blame her after what he'd witnessed so far.

'We thought you were having one of your temper tantrums and we should just leave you to it. I told you we didn't want a scene.' Evie's stepsister turned her back on them and proceeded to gather the empty champagne glasses and walk away to the kitchen. They'd apparently missed the toast and he was thankful for Evie's sake she hadn't had to go through that at least. They both might well have choked on the champagne.

'We didn't want to disturb you, dear.'

June was more diplomatic, though Jake got the impression they'd been happy to have Evie out of the way for the remainder of the party, lest she would say anything incrimi-

nating about how the happy couple came to
be together.

'How are we going to get out of here?' Evie
demanded.

'Do you have a snow shovel, Mrs Kerrigan?' Perhaps he could make some sort of
road out of here.

She shook her sleek blonde hair. 'Even if
I did, you wouldn't get out at the bottom of
the lane. It's treacherous down there, by all
accounts. Everyone else left before the snow
began. I'm afraid you're stuck here for at least
the night.'

He could only imagine how that news
was going to go down with Evie when he
felt physically sick at the prospect. After wit-
nessing their ill-treatment of her, he knew
she wouldn't want to spend a second longer
in their presence than necessary. They were
toxic, and damaging, to someone who deserved better.

He wanted to get her away from these people, but he was also worried about the consequences of this enforced stay in her company
for him too. For someone he was supposed
to be pretending to like, he'd had some very
real feelings towards her today. And not just
the physical ones he'd experienced after wak-

ing up beside her in bed. Jake already cared
enough about Evie to not want to subject her
to any more 'family time', a development he
hadn't anticipated, or wanted, when he deliberately steered away from this kind of emotional drama. He'd made the decision years
ago to only worry about himself. It was safer
than getting close to anyone. But Evie had
managed to slip past those defences and make
him feel protective towards her. Along with
everything else.

'We can't be stuck here. We can't stay here.
Jake has to get back. This wasn't the deal.'

In her panic, she'd almost let the details
of their arrangement slip. As expected, the
news had sent her into a tailspin and if her
detractors had any inkling of their 'relationship' they'd tear her to shreds. He didn't think
she could take much more. Her vulnerability
was so startlingly obvious it was no wonder
they saw her as easy prey. Jake felt it was part
of his role as her partner, fake or otherwise,
to support her. To let her know that he was
there for her, regardless of his own misgiv-
ings about their situation. They were powerless to do anything anyway.

He slipped his arms around Evie's waist
and gave her a hug to reassure her that they'd

survive this together. 'It's okay. I've nothing to rush back for. As long as we're together it'll be all right. I promise.' He did his best to reassure her they'd survive an overnight stay here, even though it was likely both of their nightmares come true.

Looking up at him with big, trusting brown eyes, Evie nodded. He knew in this moment he was the only person she had to rely on. Whilst it wasn't a position he wanted to be in, he wasn't going to let her down. Not today at least.

'Such a drama queen,' Bailey snipped, earning a dark look from Jake, and a wish that he could knock him out. But he was here to calm troubled waters, not whip them up into a storm.

'Where are we going to stay?' she asked quietly.

'Your room, of course. You seemed quite cosy there earlier. Courtney and Bailey will be in her old room. I really don't see the problem, dear.'

She wouldn't. Evie, on the other hand, was looking at him in such a state of panic he was beginning to feel it himself. That bed was tiny, and torturous. It was one thing falling asleep atop the covers by accident, but quite another being expected to share it for the night. Still, to make a big deal over it would raise suspicion and blow their cover. The last thing Evie needed.

'I'm sure we'll manage.' He rubbed her back reassuringly and felt the muscles beneath his fingertips begin to un-bunch.

'If we're all here for the night, why don't we play some board games to pass the time?'

Courtney's suggestion was met by a chorus of groans but she pouted until she got her way and everyone agreed.

So it came to be that five of them set up in the lounge, Evie and Jake against the rest, in a battle of wits, and wills. It only served to highlight the differences between Evie and her stepsister. Her general knowledge was far superior to Courtney's, much to her and Bailey's frustration. When it came to team games, guessing one another's drawing clues, Jake and Evie seemed to be in tune. Their high fives to one another was a stark contrast to the blank faces on the other team, and Bailey's frequent insults to Courtney's intelligence. In the end, with Courtney on the brink of tears, and the engagement almost over before it began, they agreed to call it a night on the game night fun.

'Why don't I make us all a nice cup of tea?' June suggested as Bailey shoved all the game contents roughly back into the boxes.

'That would be lovely, thank you.'

Jake hoped this would signal the end of their forced proximity for the night. They'd been conciliatory and sociable, and at one point he and Evie had even seemed to be enjoying the games. Probably because they'd won most of them, causing Bailey and Courtney's moods to darken considerably. He didn't care about that, only that Evie seemed more relaxed.

Of course this wasn't where he wanted to be tonight, especially overnight. He had business to tend to, and he had some concerns about how involved he was becoming in Evie's life. However, if it helped her to be more at ease with herself, and events beyond her control, it would be worthwhile.

Perhaps not wanting to be left alone with Bailey and Courtney in the living room, Evie headed into the kitchen, with Jake following close behind. He didn't trust himself not to speak his mind to those who'd betrayed her so cruelly if they should say anything more derogatory about her in his presence.

'Can we do anything to help?' Evie had

already busied herself getting the china cups and plates from the cupboard as June stirred the teapot.

'Perhaps Jake could carry the tray in? We'll put those big muscles to use.' She was teasing him but he swore Evie was blushing more than he was at the mention of his physique. It was sweet that she was embarrassed on his behalf, but he was also wondering if there was more to it. If perhaps he'd become more than a convenience to her too.

Whilst it was a complication he didn't need, it at least validated that the bond between them wasn't just all in his head.

'Evie, you take in the plate of sweet stuff,' he heard June order her behind him, noticing it wasn't often Courtney was called to do anything too taxing. Evie would oblige for the same reason she'd offered to help in the first place, because she was kind-natured, and that was the main difference between her and her family. When they spoke to her as though she was somehow inferior to them, all he wanted to do was gather her in his arms and protect her from the vitriol. Although probably not before giving them a piece of his mind first. He only held back because he knew that wasn't what she wanted. His role here was to be visibly present, and quietly supportive. Hopefully, he'd remember that and didn't manage to widen the chasm between Evie and her family even further.

Bailey and Courtney were lying nauseatingly entwined across the full length of the settee, letting June pour their tea for them.

'Would you like something to eat?' Evie offered them the plate of chocolate-covered teacakes and mince pies.

He couldn't bear to see her pander to them just to keep the peace. She was a better person than he was, that was for sure.

Courtney screwed up her nose. 'Are you trying to make me fat? I have to watch my figure. You keep them for yourself, Evie. I know you like the sweet stuff.'

Now Jake knew they were being mean to her just for the sake of it. Evie had curves in all the right places and he would rather have that than a clearly unhappy person who could only get their kicks putting other people down. Specifically, this woman whom he'd become very fond of in such a short space of time.

'I'll take one. Life's too short to count calories.' He helped himself to a teacake and popped it whole into his mouth.

To his delight, Evie copied him and they stood, laughter dancing in their eyes, munching down the sweet treats. Courtney tutted.

'Can you two sit down? I can't see the TV past you.' Bailey waved them out of the way, even though the volume had been turned way down and Jake doubted he had any real desire to watch Z-list celebrities dancing to Christmas songs. He just didn't like to see Evie happy.

With Bailey and Courtney taking up the entirety of the sofa with no attempt to make room for anyone else, Jake and Evie were forced to share one armchair. He sat in the seat and she was forced to perch on his lap. Uncomfortable for all concerned.

'Tell us where you two met.' June made an attempt at conversation even though he hoped she wouldn't probe too deep into their so-called relationship.

'We…uh…' Under the spotlight, Evie seemed to struggle with the idea of telling the story, so Jake took over.

'I popped into the studio to see about one of Evie's classes for my employees. We hit it off, and things just progressed from there.' He stayed as close to the truth as he could for now, not wanting to make Evie feel any more uncomfortable about this ruse.

'What classes?' June asked, showing she didn't know much about her stepdaughter's life at all.

Evie cleared her throat. 'I…er…run pottery and pizza evenings. I show groups how to throw their own pot, then they can order a pizza and have a drink afterwards.'

'Putting that degree to good use,' Bailey sniffed.

'The classes are very popular.' He felt the need to defend her when she had absolutely nothing to be ashamed of. On the contrary, it was apparent to Jake that Evie was a success despite her family, and had made it all on her own.

'I have to run a few different classes and things to pay the studio overheads, but I do my own range of ceramics and take commissions too.'

It was a shame Evie felt the need to defend how she made her living when it was clear to him how much she enjoyed it.

'You should be proud of her. She built a business up on her own and made a success of it. Trust me, it's not easy to do in this day and age.' He made a point of celebrating her achievements because it was about time some-one did. If that meant shaming her family into finally recognising what an amazing woman Evie was, then so be it.

'I am proud of her,' June spluttered into her tea.

'Spending all day playing in the dirt just seems a little…provincial.' It was Courtney turning her nose up at Evie's career now, and he felt her tense in his lap.

'And what is it *you* do for a living?' He couldn't help himself. They were so busy putting Evie down he doubted they had any time for self-reflection, or self-awareness.

'I'm a personal shopper at a very well-known department store, but I don't see what that has to do with anything.'

'So you spend other people's money for a living? Very admirable. I guess we're all just making our way in this world, and no one has the right to criticise how we do that. Especially if we make other people happy and get tremendous satisfaction from our work. We shouldn't let anyone try to take that away from us.' It was the closest he could get to telling them all to leave Evie alone without actually saying the words.

'I think it's probably time we went to bed.

Hopefully, the snow will have cleared by the morning and we can be on our way first thing.' Evie jumped to her feet, giving Jake a pleading look to come with her.

It was obvious she wasn't happy with him for saying what he had, but he regretted none of it. At least he had peace of mind in knowing he'd stood up for her, given her some support in the face of her family, and that was what she'd wanted him there for. Although perhaps she'd seen him in more of a non-speaking role…

'I know you've done very well for yourself, Evie. Your father would be proud of you.' Finally, June made some attempt at praising her stepdaughter. Enough to bring tears to Evie's eyes.

'Thanks. I hope so.' Her voice cracked as she reached out a hand to Jake. 'Bed?'

For a heartbeat he'd forgotten this was for everyone else's sake and took her hand, ready to sweep her off to bed. Then he remembered where they were, that this wasn't real and he wasn't going to actually spend the night how his wide-awake body was hoping.

'Oh, look. You're under the mistletoe. Isn't that sweet? A goodnight kiss before you leave.' Courtney threw one last spanner in the works before they could make their escape.

Jake looked up to find the troublesome sprig of white berries hanging from the chandelier, then at Evie, who seemed frozen to the spot. They were under scrutiny now, and though he wanted to kiss her passionately and eliminate any doubts in her family's minds that they were a couple, he was reluctant to do so. Firstly, because it wasn't something they'd discussed and he didn't want to do something as intimate as that without her permission. Also, because there were certain parts of him that didn't need any more encouragement when it came to this woman.

He leaned in, watched her eyes flutter shut and her lips part. Mustering all the strength he could find, he simply gave her a peck on the mouth, not wanting to linger there in case all of his self-control disappeared in the taste of her on his lips.

'Goodnight, everyone,' he said, not hanging around for a score on his performance, knowing it would be found lacking. However, he was willing to let his ego take a hit rather than let himself get too carried away in his role as pretend boyfriend.

None of this was real. It wouldn't do for

him to start thinking there was more to this than physical attraction, and a promise to help.

Evie needed to get out of this house now more than ever. It was bad enough being stuck here listening to her family's insults and put-downs, but now she had to lock herself away in that tiny boxroom with Jake for the night.

This evening had been emotionally over-whelming. Jake standing up for her had given her mixed feelings in that she appreciated someone doing that for the first time in her life, but confronting her family like that about their behaviour was something she'd never done. Whether he meant what he'd said or it was all part of the act she'd never know for sure. Especially when that kiss seemed to have been purely for display purposes.

If she was honest, it had been an anticli-max. When she'd known he was going to kiss her, her heart had raced in anticipation. How-ever, the reality had been rather lacklustre, to say the least. A thin-lipped, closed mouth, hard kiss which hadn't rocked her world at all. She'd expected a lot more when she'd often let her thoughts drift in that direction. The lack of passion was disappointing, and she supposed he didn't harbour any attraction towards her in the slightest. Not his fault, but it did make a mockery of the feelings she'd been having towards him when it turned out to be one-sided.

Now she had to spend the night with him, all the while knowing it was a chore for him when every touch or kind word was enough to send her pulse rocketing.

'Will you slow down.' Jake was bounding up the stairs after her and reached the bedroom just as she was closing the door.

'Sorry. I just wanted out of there.'

'It's easy to understand why. I'm so sorry you have to put up with that.'

'And you didn't help, stirring things up like that. They'll probably be ten times worse now. Don't forget there'll be a wedding to go to after all of this, and you won't be there as backup.'

The thought was disturbing. At least tonight she'd had someone to lean on. He'd been her place of sanctuary, and she knew her current attitude was a reaction to the realisation that he wasn't going to be there for ever. Nor did he want to be. That much was apparent in the awkward kiss.

'I'm sorry. I couldn't just stand back and

listen to them talk to you like that. You deserve better.'

'You can stop pretending you care, Jake. There's no one to see your performance except me.'

He frowned. 'What are you talking about? I didn't say anything I didn't mean.'

'Ah, but you do kiss women you don't want to.'

She hadn't meant to address the matter at all, but it had been bugging her that he'd clearly felt nothing in that kiss, when it seemed to Evie that she'd been waiting for it from the moment they'd met.

Another frown. 'What makes you say that? I mean, I know kissing wasn't part of our deal, but it would've looked weird if we hadn't in the circumstances. And who says I didn't want to?'

She was beginning to wish she hadn't gone down this route. Now she had to hear him say out loud that he didn't want her. Not only that, she'd have to spend the night with him in this tiny room with nowhere for either of them to hide.

'You. Your body language.'

'Trust me. I wanted to kiss you, Evie.' Standing on the other side of the room, hands in pockets, he wasn't making a convincing argument.

'Really? I'm not sure we convinced anyone with that demonstration. Don't get me wrong, I know there are men out there who don't know how to kiss properly. I just didn't expect you'd be one of them. Though I suppose when you look the way you do, you don't have to try with women…'

She was trying to reconcile what he was telling her with the experience and it just didn't add up. There had to be some reason he hadn't lived up to expectation, yet he was insisting it wasn't because of his partner. The only conclusion she could come up with was that perhaps that was simply his kissing style. Flat. Unexciting. And such a shame.

Rather than look embarrassed, shocked or angry by her review, he wore a determined expression as he crossed the floor towards her in one long stride.

'I know how to bloody kiss.'

Jake moved swiftly, cupping her face in his hands and planting his lips on hers. His mouth was firm and demanding at first, but as she relaxed into the kiss he softened against her. A tenderness which had been missing previously, and apparently had the capability of melting her bones.

He traced her bottom lip with the tip of his tongue, before dipping inside to meet her. She was lost to him, to the sensation of this kiss which was exceeding all previous expectations.

A little 'Mmm' of satisfaction slipped out that she knew she'd come to regret later. When she remembered every second of this encounter, and how she'd enjoyed him like an ice cream on a hot summer's day.

Then it was over as quickly as it had begun. He'd proved his point. And then some.

Jake took a step back so she could breathe again.

'When I kiss someone it's a promise of more to come. I didn't think either of us was ready for that.' His voice was husky, his face dark, and Evie's knees weak.

'Yeah, you were probably right.' She collapsed onto the edge of the bed.

He gave a half smile. 'It definitely wasn't anything to do with you, or my…technique.'

'I believe you.' Evie could certainly verify that last part of his statement. There was nothing wrong with his technique except for the need it awakened in her to do it again.

However, by challenging him like that, forcing him to kiss her like he meant it, she'd made things even more awkward for them.

'I don't want to make things complicated between us when the whole idea of this was to make things easier. I still need you to be my fake wedding date.' His grin went some way to helping the truth go down easier.

He was right. She was a mess. This absolutely was not the right time or place to get involved with anyone, much less the man posing as her fake boyfriend. Since he'd upheld his end of their contract she could hardly back out when he needed her to step up for him soon in return.

'Of course. Let's just put it behind us and get this night over with.'

Then they could go their separate ways until the wedding at least. A little distance and perspective would help her realise this had been nothing more than a lonely woman reading more into a kiss than was intended. It was Jake's ego at work here, not his pent-up lust for her. She'd challenged him, and he'd more than stepped up to the plate to prove himself. Now she had to get over it.

And perhaps take Ursula's advice to get

back on the singles market if she was so het-up over one little kiss.

'Where do you want me?'

She studied Jake's face for signs of amusement, convinced he was trying to rile her further, but no, he was being serious. She was the one with issues, immediately picturing him in her bed, carrying on where that kiss had left off.

'I...um...'

It would seem churlish to ask him to sleep anywhere other than the bed, given they'd shared it only hours earlier. However, she knew she was going to find it difficult lying so close to him now, her body acutely aware of how he could make her feel. The only problem was there weren't a lot of choices available in such a tiny space.

'I can take the chair if you toss me one of the pillows.' Thankfully, Jake's gallantry saw him provide the solution, no doubt at the price of his own comfort.

The egg-shaped wicker chair in the corner of her room had never been the most comfortable item of furniture in the world, but it was going to have to do for one night.

'If you're sure?' She did her best to provide some padding to soften the impact of the hard surface, kitting the inside of it out with some scatter cushions for him to sit on.

'It's fine. As soon as the snow clears, we'll be out of here anyway.'

Seeming as anxious as she was to leave, Evie imagined him sitting watching out of the window all night for the first sign of a thaw so he could get the car revving for their get-away. Which wasn't a bad thing, considering tonight's events.

Evie hunted through her old chest of drawers and pulled out an old, shapeless night-shirt with cartoon dogs plastered on the front. She wanted to be comfortable enough that she might actually be able to sleep and forget about this evening, as well as keep her clothes semi-respectable to wear again in the morning. It was doubtful she had anything in her teenage wardrobe that would fit her, or be suitable for a woman now in her late twenties. This veritable sackcloth wasn't in the least bit sexy, so any idea of passion would be killed stone dead as soon as she donned it. Maybe then they'd both be able to put all thoughts of that kiss out of their heads.

'I'm afraid I don't have anything suitable for you to wear. Unless you'd be comfortable sleeping in a pair of yoga pants and a crop top, because I'm pretty sure that's all I left in that wardrobe.' Despite the teasing, the idea of seeing him in such tight, revealing clothing was tempting.

He tightened his lips in faux outrage. 'I think I'll pass, thanks.'

Instead, he took off his jacket, undid his tie and opened the top few buttons of his shirt. He kicked off his shoes and sat back in the chair. Still pretty much clothed, Evie wondered how he managed to make it seem as though she'd just been given a strip show. It had been equally, if not more, erotic unbuttoning that formal exterior than if she'd had a greased up male exotic dancer giving her a lap dance.

She quickly disappeared into the bathroom, clutching her nightie like a shy virgin who'd just caught a glimpse of her first naked man.

A splash of cold water on her face and a change into her nightwear brought her rising temperature down a little, but it wouldn't stop the indecent thoughts she kept having about him. It was only when she exited the bathroom and his cool gaze followed her across the room that she realised how short the nightdress was on her adult body now. It appeared the attraction went both ways.

She didn't think the effort he'd put into that kiss was entirely an act to salve his fragile ego. Still, taking things any further than one kiss wasn't a good move for either of them. They needed each other for more than the short-lived pleasure she might gain from a fling, because he'd made it clear he didn't do relationships. Though Evie wasn't ready to get into any sort of serious commitment either, she doubted anything casual was going to do her any good.

If she ever ventured into sharing her life, or her heart, with anyone again, it would have to be with someone she knew was going to be there for her. A man who thought she was enough, and wouldn't need to look elsewhere. Someone she could trust not to let her down and break her heart. Jake had been upfront with her about the kind of man he was. A workaholic who'd been prepared to give up a loving, long-term relationship for a business deal. There was absolutely nothing to be gained from thinking about him in any sort of romantic scenario.

So why couldn't she stop?

CHAPTER FIVE

JAKE WOKE EARLY, having spent half the night replaying events in his head, and squirming in the most uncomfortable chair he'd ever had the misfortune to sit in.

Evie, on the other hand, looked quite content sleeping in her bed, and he was reluctant to wake her. She deserved that tiny bit of peace.

Slowly and carefully, he picked his way across the floor to the window, trying not to wake her. He took a peek outside. It was beginning to rain now and hopefully by the time Evie stirred they'd be able to make tracks through what was left of the snow. He eased the door open, taking one last look at her lying there, hair mussed and that damned nightshirt riding high on her thighs. The very reason he had to get out of this room.

He'd inflicted a special kind of torture on himself by kissing her like that last night. He could pretend he was making a point, defending his honour and reputation, but that hadn't been his main motivation. It was simply the excuse he'd needed to kiss Evie the way he wanted, without an audience. Now he was going to be plagued for ever with the knowledge of how she felt in his arms, tasted on his tongue and responded passionately to him in return. Everything he didn't need to know if he was going to be able to go ahead with this wedding date charade.

Goodness knew he wasn't looking to get any more involved with Evie and her family than he already was. He had to stick to the plan. No strings. No complications. No kissing.

Evie had obviously had her heart broken and was carrying way more emotional baggage than he needed in his life. The last thing she would be ready for was a man whose work was his priority, and who had no idea of settling down. She wasn't going to have her heart mended by him, a man who'd left her in bed to come downstairs and catch up on the work he'd missed out on. Because that was his life, the only dependable thing in it that no one could take away from him.

Jake made his way into the kitchen and

made himself a coffee. He liked this time of morning when everything was still. As if the rest of the world was yet to wake. Even the birds were still in their slumber. It helped quieten his mind for a little while. Until his thoughts were consumed with work and ensuring that he, and everyone working for him, had a secure future.

Taking his coffee to the kitchen table, he sat down and video-called Donna. Like him, she'd be awake and raring to go. Another crossover from life with an army parent who'd made sure they did their chores before they even left the house for school in the mornings.

The call had barely connected before Donna's face appeared on the screen. She was already dressed, hair perfect and make-up immaculate. Jake was definitely slacking today.

'Hi, bro. Where are you? I know it's Sunday but you're usually in the office by now. It's a bit rich expecting me to come in if you're not going to be here.' She was peering behind him, trying to figure out where he was, clearly miffed that she'd had to give up her Sunday morning lie-in for this important meeting they had with a film company. Unfortunately, it was the only day Jake had been able to make work.

'I know. I got snowed in. I'll get there as soon as I can, but I need to get home and shower first. Can you manage things until I get there?'

It was a rhetorical question. He knew as well as she did that his little sister was every bit as capable as he was of running the business. She simply chose a life over work. Sometimes he wondered if she had the right idea, working to live rather than living to work. He imagined if Evie was in his bed every morning, he might find it harder to leave the house.

'Of course. Wait… You haven't been home? You dirty stop-out.'

'It's not like that. I was doing a friend a favour and I got trapped because of the weather. Otherwise, I would've been home and we wouldn't be having this phone call.'

'A friend, eh?'

Her grin was nauseating, but he knew she was only teasing because he never let her meet anyone he spent the night with. Apart from the fact his private life had nothing to do with her, he didn't want her to know about Evie and get the wrong idea. It wasn't as though they'd actually slept together. At least not in the way his sister would probably imagine. A scenario he was trying to avoid.

'Yes.' He adopted his serious, don't-mess-with-me boss face, ignoring the fact he was wearing yesterday's wrinkled clothes and hadn't washed, shaved or brushed his hair today. Something which was blatantly obvious, seeing himself on the screen. He looked like he'd spent the night half sleeping in a chair wondering what new mess he'd got himself into.

'I hope you'll be bringing this "friend" to the wedding so I can meet her.'

Jake just knew he was never going to hear the end of this. It was such a novelty for him to be caught on the hop like this, Donna was going to use it against him at every given opportunity, like any little sister would.

'Listen, I need you to host my nine o'clock meeting. You have all the facts and figures there. Just tell them I'll catch up with them when I'm back at my desk.' He chose to ignore the teasing and try to refocus her on the more important business at hand. His absence was unprofessional, and it didn't sit well with him, even if it was a source of amusement for Donna.

'Sorry. I didn't realise you were down here.

I thought you'd left without me.' A sleepy Evie walked into shot in her tiny nightdress and completely blew all pretence of credibility for him with his sister.

'I'll talk to you later, Donna.'

Jake ended the call. Too late for him to possibly have any valid excuse for why he'd spent the night here with Evie. Not least because she was going to be his plus one at the wedding. He supposed it gave his story more credibility, but he didn't want Donna to think he was distracted from his job.

Evie's hand went to her mouth. 'I'm so sorry. I didn't know you were on a call. I can go back upstairs if you like?'

'It's okay. I was just letting them know I'd be late into the office this morning. I didn't want to wake you. I would never have gone without you.'

As tempting as it might have been to get in the car and drive far away from the situation he'd got himself into, Jake would never have done that to her. He didn't want to be another one to let her down and break the trust she'd shown in him by even bringing him here.

'Do you need to go now? Sorry, I didn't realise you'd be working today. I can throw my clothes on.'

She still had that dreamy look on her face, her hair a tangled curtain around her pale face. He could see she needed a little time to come round before they made a hasty exit.

'It's okay. Donna is going to take care of things until I get in. Take your time and have some breakfast. You didn't have much to eat last night.'

Neither had he, but he was used to working through the night on meagre sustenance. Evie should take the opportunity to have some food without every morsel being analysed and commented on. At least she might be able to enjoy it without a critical audience.

'I am hungry.' Evie hunted in the cupboards looking for something to eat, and finally settled on a box of cereal.

Jake did his best to look away when she stretched up to get a bowl, her nightshirt revealing even more of her soft thighs and the curve of her backside, and failed.

'Would you like some?' She turned to meet his gaze.

He blinked, then realised she was talking about breakfast. 'No, thanks.'

Okay, so maybe he would chivvy her along after she'd eaten, and get back to real life.

Where he wasn't tempted by half naked women distracting him from work.

Evie brought her breakfast over to sit at the table with him.

'Was it an important call? I know you're a busy man. Sorry you're stuck here.'

'I had a meeting this morning, but Donna's going to take care of it until I get there. These things happen. It's no one's fault.'

If anyone was to blame, it was him. He should never have lain down on that bed with her. He'd crossed the line between being an anonymous fake boyfriend and being someone who cared about her. Now he was suffering the consequences.

'Your sister's very pretty.'

If Evie had time to see Donna, that meant in all likelihood she'd spotted Evie too. At the very least she'd heard her. Jake groaned inwardly, knowing the teasing and one hundred and one questions he'd face when he got home.

'Pretty annoying,' he answered back, in that childlike tone siblings always adopted when talking about one another.

'Yet you work together?'

'I didn't say she wasn't good at her job. She knows me better than anyone, and compensates in areas where I'm apparently found lacking. Hence the suggestion for the pottery night in the first place. Apparently, I'm intimidating and distant.'

Evie didn't contradict him.

'Donna likes to think she's the friendly face of the company. I don't know what that says about me.'

'You do have a certain…do not approach vibe. But I know beyond that there's a very caring man, willing to stand up for someone he barely knows in front of her family.'

He didn't know how to cope with the unexpected praise, so he quietly accepted it.

'Donna moved with me when I was setting up the business. Said there was nothing keeping her in London any more. I think she'd just split up with her latest boyfriend. She's another romantic, I'm afraid.'

Although Donna's attitude towards relationships was slightly different to his. She wasn't afraid to get involved with anyone, but she had a habit of moving on quickly when it didn't work out. A product of their nomadic upbringing, he feared.

'At least you get along, are there for each other. I often wonder what it would've been like to have had a full sibling. You know, someone who didn't mind that I was part of their life.'

Jake took Donna for granted, both as a sister and as a valued member of staff. He couldn't imagine being without her, or her treating him the way Courtney treated Evie. Naturally, they teased each other, like all siblings, but it was usually in good humour. She was really the only person he had in the world to confide in, to lean on. The only person he could rely on in life. Evie didn't even have that with her stepsister. It was no wonder that she was lonely.

'You won't want to hang around much longer then, will you?' Although he'd told her to take her time, now Jake was beginning to think they should get on the move as soon as possible. Not that he was looking forward to facing Donna, who wasn't going to let this matter drop, but at least he and Evie could get some distance between them again.

'I'll get dressed. I'd prefer to get out of here before anyone else gets up. I'll leave a note.' Evie rinsed her dishes and put them back in the cupboard, before going back upstairs to get changed. With any luck they'd be on their way soon and be able to put all this behind them.

Jake only hoped by the time the wedding

came around they'd have forgotten all about what had happened. That he'd have put it from his mind how it felt to share a bed with her and forget the outside world existed.

'So…?'

'"So" what?' Jake ignored Donna, hovering in his office doorway, and went straight to his desk and logged on his computer.

'Who is she?'

'Who's who?' He played dumb, not wanting to place any significance on the woman he'd been with, and give Donna ammunition.

She rolled her eyes at him and followed him over to his desk. Clearly, she wasn't going to let the matter drop.

'The woman you were obviously with last night. The woman I saw wearing next to nothing on the call this morning.'

'Why are you so interested? I don't quiz you on your love life.'

'Because, dear brother, I have never known you to be late for work on account of a woman. Never mind stay over at their place.'

'I told you. We were snowed in,' he said weakly.

'Uh-huh. And are we going to meet this

mystery woman at any point? Will she be going to the wedding?'

This was exactly what he'd been dreading. That Donna was going to put two and two together and he was going to end up with a wife.

'Yes, she's going to the wedding, but don't get too carried away, okay? We've just met.' There was little point in denying everything when he was supposed to be convincing people that they were a couple for the wedding. He just didn't want anyone thinking they were in a serious relationship.

'What's her name?'

'Evie. Now, how did you get on without me this morning?' He did his best to change the subject now she'd got as much information out of him as he was willing to give.

'Fine. Although they probably won't believe anything until they speak to the *real* boss. Now, back to more important matters… When will I get to meet this Evie?'

Jake let out a frustrated breath. 'At the wedding. Don't make a big deal out of it, please, Donna. I just like her company.'

That much was true. Well, there was a lot more than that which he appreciated about her, but he needed to downplay it for this conversation.

'It is a big deal. I don't know the last time I even saw you with a woman, and the fact you're bringing her to the wedding…'

'Don't read anything into that. It's just to stop Mum matchmaking with every single woman within a hundred-mile radius for me.'

'I'm just happy for you, Jake.'

To his horror, she rushed around the desk and grabbed him into a side hug. He eventually managed to shrug her off.

'Yes, I'm happy for me too. Now, can we get back to work?'

He gave up trying to deny anything else when Donna was as stubborn as he was at times. The only way to get rid of her was to tell her she was right. It did the trick.

'Okay, bro. If you're not going to tell me anything else I'll get back to work. I'll just have to get to know Evie at the wedding.'

Why did that sound like a threat?

His thoughts turned to Evie at the wedding and being ambushed by his sister. She definitely wasn't ready for that. Even though he'd left her less than an hour ago he found himself calling her number. He had to warn her, right?

As he waited for her to answer, he realised he'd been in the office ten minutes and he hadn't opened his emails or checked his calendar. He was definitely changing already and Donna wasn't the only one he needed to be careful didn't carried away.

The only reason he was calling Evie now was so she didn't get caught out in their lie at the wedding. It would be humiliating for both of them. He would give her some warning about what she was in for, then leave her alone until the wedding. Once that was over, their arrangement done, they never had to see each other again. It didn't have to be the crisis he was anticipating simply because he'd enjoyed kissing her.

'Hello?' The sound of Evie's voice immediately soothed his troubled mind.

'Evie? It's Jake.'

'Is everything all right?' Her concern was palpable and he felt better that she worried for him the way he'd done about her last night.

'Yes, I just wanted to give you a heads-up that since catching a glimpse of you this morning, my sister is very eager to get to know you. Don't worry, I'll try to head her off as much as possible at the wedding but I thought I'd prepare you.'

Silence.

'Evie? Did you hear me?'

'Yes,' she answered quietly. 'About the wedding… I'm wondering if it's a good idea at all for us to go together.'

Jake's stomach dropped onto the floor. He'd clearly crossed the line somewhere when she was backing out already. It could be down to the fact he was already phoning her after just having dropped her off home, or it could be because he'd kissed her when there was no call for it. He hadn't realised how much he'd been looking forward to seeing her again already until it might not be a possibility at all.

'Is something wrong?'

What did I do?

'It's just a lot. I'm not very good at social situations, as you've seen for yourself. I don't know what to wear, and I'm likely to embarrass you as much as myself. You'd be better going without me. Which reminds me, I still have your credit card. You're going to need that back. Maybe I can courier it over to you.' She was tripping over her words in her haste to get them out. It reminded Jake of that first night in her studio when she'd charmed him into agreeing to this ridiculous situation in the first place.

'It's fine. I have plenty of others. Hold onto it in case you change your mind. I would really like you to be with me, Evie. Listen, if it's the dress code that's bothering you, maybe I can make time to go with you to find something suitable if you like? We could grab some lunch too. What do you say?'

Jake couldn't quite believe he was offering to go shopping with her, and completely slacking where work was concerned. Yet at the moment it seemed more important to have her onside for this wedding where he'd have to face his parents. He was beginning to think it was more about having the support than convincing his family he was happily settled with someone. Being there for Evie last night seemed to have made a difference and helped her get through a difficult evening, and he was hoping for the same.

If all it took to get Evie to accompany him was to play hooky from work for a couple of hours and get her a dress, it would be worth it.

The silence on the other end of the line seemed to go on way too long. Until eventually she offered an unenthusiastic, 'Sure.'

It was enough to satisfy Jake for now. Though if Donna found out he'd never hear the end of it.

* * *

Evie didn't know how on earth she was going to stomach lunch when her whole body was tense and tied in knots. Including her head. She'd decided against going to the wedding with Jake even before he'd called to warn her that his sister would likely give her the third degree over their alleged relationship.

It had been a week since the engagement party but, unable to get that kiss out of her head, or the way she'd caught him looking at her that morning with undisguised lust, she'd thought better of seeing him again. But here she was, already going against all common sense to meet up with him only days later.

After dealing with Courtney and Bailey her emotions were in turmoil, and this attraction she was feeling towards Jake wasn't helping. She thought he might have been glad to get out of their arrangement and used her outfit as a lame excuse to call things off. Jake had called her bluff, apparently still keen for her to accompany him to his mother's wedding. How could she let him down when he'd done so much for her?

There was also the matter of her wanting to see him again. Usually, she was more than happy holed up in her studio, avoiding the world outside and anything, or anyone, that could possibly hurt her. However, she knew part of the tension inside came from the anticipation of spending more time with Jake. The only person in a long time who'd stood up for her, worried about her...taken care of her. Perhaps she was mistaking that for something more that had been missing from her life since she'd found out that Bailey was cheating on her, but she enjoyed being with Jake. That feeling had been missing for too long in her life, and even if it only lasted until his mum's wedding was over, she would take it.

As Evie turned the corner onto Royal Avenue an icy wind blasted, her long padded black coat proving scant protection from the cold. She pulled her scarf up over her nose and mouth and strode against the blustery weather. When she saw Jake standing on the pavement ahead waiting for her, her temperature shot up a few degrees.

'Hey. Thanks for coming.' He greeted her with a kiss on the cheek and his warmth, though short-lived, helped to thaw her a little more.

'I should be thanking you. You're the one who'll be paying,' she teased, trying to keep this about fulfilling her promise to him by attending his mother's wedding.

'I thought we could try a few boutique shops I've heard Donna talking about. Failing that, we can get a personal shopper to help us.'

He was scrolling on his phone, clearly having researched some suitable stores. It was touching that he'd taken it upon himself to come with her when he could easily have sent someone in his place. He was a busy man after all. Perhaps he just wanted to make sure she wouldn't back out again.

'As long as it's not Courtney! I'm happy to have a look first. I'm not sure how comfortable I'd be with a personal shopper.' Apart from the expense involved, the idea of a polished, sophisticated store assistant measuring her up, and bustling into the changing room with her, wasn't something she'd look forward to.

'I'm no expert but I can give you my opinion, as well as my credit card.' Jake grinned and linked his arm through hers.

It might well have been a tactic to stop her from running away, but Evie relished the close body contact, regardless that it was how he made her feel that had given her second thoughts about the wedding. The experts always said treats in moderation didn't do a body any harm…

'I like that one on you.' Jake's eyes lit up when Evie stepped out of the changing room wearing a multicoloured mid-length dress which nipped in at her waist and had a daring plunging neckline.

'You're no help. You like all of them.' She rolled her eyes and smiled.

'Exactly. You look good in anything, so just pick the one you feel most comfortable in.'

Clothes shopping was usually a chore, even when it came to choosing for himself, but he'd enjoyed sitting here having his own private fashion show. Evie was shy about her body, probably as a result of her ex's betrayal. The rejection she must have felt would undoubtedly have had an effect on her self-esteem when she was such a sensitive soul. But she had absolutely no need to worry on that score. She was beautiful, inside and out. Bailey was an idiot for ever letting her go.

'Well, it's not this one. I'd be too afraid of falling out of it.' She was tugging at the two strips of fabric currently covering her modesty.

'We can rule that out then. Next.'

He sat back and waited, hoping she was secretly enjoying this as much as he was. It was probably a long time since anyone had treated her to anything, judging by her family. Anything she had, she'd worked for herself. Much like him. She deserved a little spoiling. Goodness knew he wasn't averse to splurging money on himself when the mood took him.

'I'm not sure about this one either...' She opened the curtain tentatively and stepped out, taking Jake's breath away in the process.

The blush pink silk skimmed the curve of her hips, and the slit at the side showed off her long lean legs when she moved.

'Stunning,' he said, once he remembered to close his mouth.

'It's very tight though. One canapé too many and it might burst at the seams. It shows everything.'

She had that right. Under the air-conditioning he could see that the cold was reaching her extremities. The last thing either of them wanted was to have people staring at her hardened nipples. Including Jake.

'What about the first one you tried on? We both liked it.' Anything to take his mind off her perky breasts and stop him feeling like a voyeur.

'Give me a second.' She hitched up the skirt and waddled back into the cubicle, re-emerging with a smile on her face.

'Yes. You look beautiful in that too.' It was a modest white sheath dress emblazoned with a cobalt blue trailing leaf which reminded him of the Willow Pattern china his mother used to have. Nothing special on its own, but it showed off Evie's figure without being too revealing. The most attractive feature was the beaming smile she was wearing with it.

'I think this is the one. Though I'm afraid I might be too cold. It is December after all.'

As if by magic, the shop assistant appeared with matching accessories. 'We have a bolero-style jacket or a stunning blue cashmere pashmina, which will go perfectly with that.'

'Oh, that's beautiful.' Evie stroked the pashmina with longing, and the assistant launched into her sales spiel.

'You can wear it as a shawl or a wrap.' She draped the fabric around Evie's shoulders and she snuggled into it.

'It's so soft,' Evie sighed, clearly in love.

Not about to waste an opportunity, another assistant arrived with a matching clutch bag, shoes and hat. The pair set to work kitting

Evie out in the full outfit, and she was beaming in the midst of it all.

'Sold,' he said, much to everyone's apparent glee.

'We also have a matching tie.' One of the sales women ran off to fetch a silk tie for him to co-ordinate with his wedding date.

'Yes. Fine. Add that to the bill too.'

'Oh, Jake. Let me get that for you. It's the least I can do,' Evie pleaded, taking the tie for herself.

'There's no need.' He knew she was probably on a limited budget which likely didn't include expensive silk ties.

'Please. I want to.' Those pleading eyes were too hard to resist. He knew this was more about the gesture than the cost.

'If you insist.'

'I do.' She disappeared back into the changing room to take off the outfit before he could argue any further.

As the sales assistants carried her purchases to the till, Evie cradled the tie in her hands as though it was the most expensive item in the store.

Jake appreciated that she wanted to do something for him. Too often people took it for granted that he would pay for a meal or a taxi, because of who and what he was. Although he didn't mind covering any bills, he did mind when people expected it from him. When they didn't appreciate him for who he was, and thought more about what they could do for him. Evie was different. This was her way of saying thanks, and showing him that they were in this together. Even though she was the one doing him a favour by attending the event of the year.

'So…lunch? Where would you like to go? There's a good tasting menu on at the hotel I usually take my clients to for dinner.' At least he had plenty of experience when it came to impressing people with good food and fine wine. He reckoned they deserved it after a busy morning of shopping.

To his astonishment, Evie turned her nose up at the idea of a posh meal in a fancy restaurant.

'Could we get something on the go? The Christmas Market is on at City Hall and I never get the chance to go there. They have loads of food stalls there. I'd love to have a walk around and soak up the atmosphere. Unless you'd rather not? I don't want to keep you from anything more important.'

'There's nothing that can't wait.' Presently, he couldn't think of anything he'd rather do.

They put their purchases in the car and walked the short distance to City Hall, where the grounds were alive with Saturday Christmas shoppers and the air was filled with amazing aromas coming from the food stalls. The Salvation Army band outside the gates was playing traditional Christmas carols, adding to the whole festive atmosphere.

'I think I'll get a hot chocolate to try and warm up. Can I get you one?' Evie stopped at the first log cabin style stall selling all manner of hot beverages, including mulled wine and spiced cider.

'I'll take a hot chocolate too, thanks. You can have a shot of whiskey or brandy in yours to really warm you up. If I wasn't driving, I might have been tempted...'

Evie frowned. 'And spoil the taste of my hot chocolate? No, thanks.'

She ordered their drinks, which arrived quickly, and they carried their takeaway cups with them as they browsed the other stalls. A variety of sweet treats, wooden and knitted crafts, artisan soaps and personalised Christmas decorations, there was plenty for everyone. There was even a mini funfair in the grounds for small children to enjoy.

'I had no idea there was so much here.'

'Have you never been before?' Evie asked, sipping her hot chocolate.

He shook his head. 'Too busy. Besides, Christmas was never really a big deal for me.'

'Why not?' Evie was looking at him as though he'd committed a crime.

'We were never in one place long enough to really get excited about the build-up to it. There were no family heirloom ornaments to decorate a tree, although I think my mother would've liked that. She goes a bit overboard now when she's decorating for the season. I think she's overcompensating. Dad didn't like us having too many unnecessary "things" because it would've made moving around more difficult. He was what you would call a minimalist.'

That was putting it mildly. He and Donna had known better than to get attached to anything because their father would've got rid of it in time for the next transfer. Therefore, Christmas presents were kept to a minimum too.

'That's awful. I can honestly say it's the one time of the year I always felt happy. Dad made such a fuss. Even June was a bit more human around Christmas. Although there was always a distinction made between Courtney and me in terms of gifts, obviously.'

'Of course.' That was how people like Evie's stepmother liked to keep control, keep her stepdaughter in her place. He could imagine her being treated as a second-class citizen next to her stepsister because he'd witnessed it for himself. He was only glad she had some good memories of her father to hold on to.

'I still have some of the tree decorations Dad and I bought before he remarried. June thought they were tacky, but her loss was my gain.'

'I suppose you're one of these people who've had their tree up since the start of December?' He was teasing, but he liked that she still had some of that childlike wonder about the season which he'd never been allowed to cultivate.

'Try November,' she said with a laugh. 'Usually. Except I've been so busy with commissions this year I haven't had a chance to get one yet. Otherwise, it would look like Santa's Grotto at my place.'

Jake didn't doubt it when she'd forgone an expensive meal out to revel in the festivities here, despite the noise and crowds. It was nice to see her happy and relaxed, simply being herself, without having to prove herself to a family that clearly didn't deserve her loyalty.

'I don't usually bother.'

'That does not surprise me.'

'Donna makes an effort in the office for the employees' sake, and she deals with corporate cards and gifts. Otherwise, it hardly registers on my radar.'

Evie was shaking her head. 'You poor, poor man. You've missed out on so much.'

'Like what? I'm usually force-fed a huge Christmas dinner by my mother, and partake in the exchanging of gifts under duress. I think that covers all the bases.'

'You make it sound like a chore. Don't you know it's the most wonderful time of the year? I suppose you don't line up all your favourite Christmas movies to watch, or eat an entirely chocolate based diet for the month?'

'Um…no.'

'When it was just the two of us at home, Dad made Christmas magical. There were so many lights on the house you could probably have seen it from space! He paid just as much attention to the inside of the house too, with decorations everywhere and our stockings hanging on the mantelpiece. It looked like a Christmas card scene. Then there was the food… My goodness, he baked gingerbread and cookies along with Christmas cakes. He read me Christmas stories every night and we used to drive around to look at everyone else's light displays. I loved that. He must have scouted those places out first because he seemed to know where the houses with the best displays were. We'd be driving in complete darkness, drinking hot chocolate, then, all of a sudden, the skies would be lit up with these amazing scenes. I don't know if he was trying to make up for Mum not being there, but he made it a special time for me growing up.'

'It does sound idyllic, but I'm guessing it didn't stay that way?' Jake saw the dip in her shoulders when other, probably more unhappy, memories were brought to the fore.

'June didn't like the tacky decorations and Courtney thought all of our little traditions were childish. I suppose they were, but that's what made it fun. Dad always made me feel like a little girl at Christmas. Until he remarried and I guess he had other priorities.' Despite having every right to feel bitter about the change in the family dynamic, Evie simply sounded sad about it.

'And you like to recreate that kind of Christmas atmosphere to remember your father.' It was a mark of Evie's resilience that she'd been able to cling on to some of those happier memories rather than focus on the negative ones her stepfamily had created.

'Yes. I know it sounds sad when I'm on my own and there's no one else to benefit from the over-the-top decorations and traditions, but that was a happy time for me. It's all I have left of my father.'

'Maybe one day you'll get to share those traditions with a family of your own.' For her sake, he hoped she would when it was clear she was desperate to recreate that happy family that had been taken away from her. He had no such inclinations.

She shrugged. 'In an ideal world, probably. But I can't see me ever wanting to get close enough to anyone for that to be a possibility. It's hard for me to trust these days.'

'I get that, but don't rule it out completely. Christmas might not be my thing, but you seem to revel in the festivities. It seems to make you happy.'

'It does.' She gave him a beaming smile. 'You don't know what you're missing out on, Jake.'

For the first time he could remember, he did actually wonder. He imagined it could be a magical time with someone like Evie. If he ever decided it wasn't just an excuse to do as little work as possible. Nothing much changed for him in that department, except his workforce and input dropped. He used the time to catch up on paperwork or prepare for the forthcoming business plans for the next year. It never entered his head to lie around like a couch potato, gorging on snacks. Although if Evie invited him to do so with her, he might be tempted.

His father hadn't been the type to encourage those whimsical notions that most children were allowed to indulge in at Christmas, or any other time of the year. But hearing Evie recall those memories with her father and seeing her smile showed how happy it made her. He wouldn't want to take any of that away from her.

'We'll have to agree to disagree on that one.'

They explored a little more around the market, sampled a few of the exotic foods available, and indulged in some sweet Dutch mini pancakes dusted with icing sugar and topped with cream. She really was a bad influence. But he was having fun.

He couldn't remember the last time he'd kicked back like this and just let himself enjoy the moment. A whole month of this with Evie was something he couldn't possibly comprehend, but he was sure he could probably come around to her way of doing things if given half a chance. Here, neither of them was worrying about work or family, or the expectations people put upon them. It seemed a simpler, happier way to exist.

Evie's phone rang then, and she moved over to the side of the grounds to answer it. He watched her face turn into a mask of concern and immediately knew something was wrong.

'Ursula? Calm down. What's wrong? Is he okay? Where is he? I'll get there as soon as I can.'

It was frustrating hearing only one side of the conversation, knowing something had happened but powerless until she hung up and recounted the conversation, which was clearly disturbing her.

Eventually she ended the call, visibly upset.

'Evie, what's wrong?'

'It's Dave—my dog. Ursula was looking after him in the studio, but he got out onto the main road. He's been hurt... I need to get to him.'

She dumped her takeaway cup in the nearest bin and rushed towards the exit.

'Evie, wait. Where is he? I can take you.' He expected her to protest that she didn't want to impose any more on him, that she would let him get back to work.

Instead, she simply said, 'At the vet's. Thank you.'

It showed how much her pet meant to her when her entire focus shifted onto his welfare.

'We'll get there as soon as we can,' he assured her as they hurried back to his car.

She was unusually quiet and he knew it was likely because she was imagining the worst, worried she wouldn't get to her dog in time. As they buckled into the car and he typed the address into the sat nav, he reached across and gave her hand a squeeze, forcing her to look at him.

'It'll be okay.'

It was a big promise, but he was going to be there for her whatever happened. He knew how important her canine companion was to her and, as far as he could tell, she didn't have anyone else in her life to give her the kind of emotional support she needed right now.

Despite his previous reservations about getting too close to her, he was willing to set them aside in order to provide a shoulder for her to lean on over the next few hours.

CHAPTER SIX

'Everything will be all right. I'll be here when you wake up.' Evie kissed her best boy's golden fur, his little whimpers breaking her heart.

'We'll phone you as soon as he's out of surgery. Hopefully, it will be straightforward but, as you know, there are always risks with older dogs when they're under anaesthetic.' The vet was as sympathetic as she could be, but Evie knew she still had to outline any possible complications.

'Thank you,' she said, doing her best to hold the tears back.

By the time she and Jake had arrived at the surgery, Dave had already been X-rayed and they'd discovered a small fracture in his back leg. She'd excused Ursula, who was almost as distraught as she was over the accident, and Jake had sat with her until the vet had come out to update her on Dave's condition. Now it was a waiting game.

'Where do you want to go now?' Jake asked gently. He'd been so kind. Not only had he bought her those beautiful, expensive clothes, and indulged her trip to the Christmas market, but he'd been there to reassure her from the moment she'd heard about Dave getting hit by a car.

They'd been having a lovely morning up until that phone call. Even though she'd pushed him out of his usual schedule, and comfort zone, he seemed to have enjoyed it as much as she had. It reminded her what it was like to have a partner to do nice things with. She hadn't had that since Bailey, and even now those memories seemed tainted by his betrayal, as though he'd been play-acting all those times they'd been happy together, and had secretly been wishing he was with Courtney.

Maybe if she could get past those intrusive thoughts, those fears that someone else would hurt her the way he had, she might be able to be happy with someone else. One day she might be ready to share her life again, and revel in those joyful moments. However, even today she knew they weren't real when Jake was only in her life because of the deal they'd made. He wasn't a potential life partner, he was simply an extended fake date, with her because she owed him.

'I don't want to go home. I need to keep busy, so I think I'll just head back to the studio. Sorry for dragging you into this, Jake.'

'It's fine. I'll stay with you until they call you.'

'You don't have to do that.'

Whilst she appreciated the offer, she didn't want him to feel obliged. Especially when he'd already gone so far out of his way today to accommodate her.

'I know, but I want to. You shouldn't be on your own. Maybe you could put me to work and I can make myself useful.'

She knew there was little he could do in the way of her commissions, but she wasn't in the right headspace to do anything of any real importance. Although it might be fun to show him how to use the wheel, perhaps give him a pottery lesson while they waited. It would certainly help take her mind off her poor boy lying on the operating table.

'You're very welcome to stop by, but if you need to go at any point I'll understand.' That at least gave him an out if he found it was eating too much into his working day. Then she wouldn't have to feel guilty about keeping Jake from his work, as well as leaving Dave this morning.

'I want to make sure the old boy is okay as well,' he said, showing that he'd already become attached to her furry companion in the short space of time he'd had with him. She assumed he was a doggy person, even though his immaculate clothes suggested someone who would avoid contamination of animal hair on his person at any cost.

'I wouldn't have had you pinned as an animal-lover.'

'I don't suppose I ever had the chance to find out. Obviously, we weren't allowed pets growing up, and I'm so busy now it wouldn't be fair to have a dog I didn't have time to take care of.'

'I was lucky. Dad was a dog-lover and we had a lovely big Bernese mountain dog called Bran when I was growing up. I was devastated when he died, but then Dad met June and she was allergic to animal hair, so we never had any more pets after that. The first thing I did when I left Bailey was go to the rescue home and pick Dave so I had someone to come home to every night.' It was a shame

Jake had never had the companionship of a pet growing up when his childhood sounded so disruptive.

'I'm glad you have him, and he's a lucky dog to have found a home with you.' Jake was so understanding, when Evie knew a lot of people would find her distress over a dog over the top. Despite never being a pet owner himself, he seemed to relate to her attachment. She supposed that was simply down to his compassionate nature, but having someone she could talk to so freely without fear of ridicule made her well up all over again.

'It must seem silly getting so upset over a pet, but he's more than that. He's a friend, a companion, and I don't know what I'd do without him.' Perhaps it was because she felt as though she was in a safe space with Jake, free to express her emotions, but the tears began to fall in earnest now.

'I know how much he means to you, and I'm sure he's going to be all right.'

When the words came from him, Evie was inclined to believe it. Jake was a steadying presence in her life, remarkable for someone who'd apparently gone through so much upheaval in his. She only hoped she could offer the same support to him some day.

They pulled up outside the studio, and when they reached the top of the staircase she almost expected to hear the pad of Dave's paws across the floor to meet her. Unfortunately, behind the door was her cold, empty studio. She'd told Ursula to go home for the day, and now she was glad Jake had insisted on coming with her.

The first things she did was turn on the radio to interrupt the silence she was worried would set her off again when she was so used to hearing Dave wrestling with his toys or appealing to her for attention.

'So, what can I do?' Jake asked, clasping his hands together as he surveyed the room.

'Um…first things first, you'll need to put an apron on.' She was worried even being in this room would ruin his suit so she lifted one of the long aprons and hung it around his neck, leaving him to tie it around his waist.

'What are you working on at the moment?'

'I have a few orders in for bespoke dinner services, and I'm trying to get some stock together for upcoming Christmas markets.'

'And obviously you want a few Jake Hanley originals in there to increase the value.'

'Obviously. Would you like to try your hand at throwing a pot?'

If she wasn't going to be able to focus on getting her work done today, she might as well try and have a little fun. It had to be better than sitting around moping, staring at pictures of her dog and wondering what she would do if the worst happened to him.

'Let's not call it a pot in case it ends up more of a modern art sculpture,' he joked, following her over to the wheel.

'Okay, put your legs either side. Like that.' She fetched one of the balls of clay ready for working with and handed it to him. 'I want you to smack that down in the centre of the wheel.'

Jake did as instructed, hitting the target and centring the clay perfectly.

'You'll need plenty of water to help form the clay.' She scooped water from the bucket beside the wheel to saturate it.

'Do I need to keep my hands wet?' he asked.

'Yes, and the wheel. If you just lean your foot on the pedal, we'll get a nice steady pace for you to work at. Good.' Now came the tricky part.

'Lean your arms on the tops of your legs to stabilise them. Lock them in. Yes, like that.' She made sure he was comfortable with the positioning before she moved onto the next step.

'Now, with both hands around the clay, keeping it centred, we want to raise it up until it resembles a traffic cone.'

Slowly, Jake pulled the wet clay up into a questionable shape which made him snigger as the tip wobbled unsteadily.

Ignoring any attempt at childish innuendo, Evie carried on with her instruction. 'Using the flat of your fist, push it down until it looks like a hockey puck shaped disc.'

She had to admit Jake was very good at following the steps, his strong hands already commanding the clay when other students were hesitant at first. He had a confidence that would likely make him a very good potter if he ever thought about taking it up on a more permanent basis.

'More water?' he asked, pausing for her consent before dousing the wheel again.

'Using both thumbs, I want you to push down slightly into the middle, careful not to go right through the bottom.'

Jake tentatively opened up a divot in the clay and, with her hands covering his, she gently guided him, pulling the walls out and up until it resembled a bowl shape. She tried not to think about the strong hands that had held her not so long ago, or what they would feel like on other parts of her body. Though this impromptu pottery lesson was definitely helping take her mind off other matters.

'It's actually starting to look like something.' His enthusiasm was touching as they drew the sides up and gave the bowl some shape. He looked at her with eyes aglow and a smile on his lips. Evie wished he took more time to enjoy the smaller things in life when he'd got such pleasure from simple things today. She wondered if he was afraid to stand still in case he realised, like her, that outside of work his life was quite empty.

Evie understood that perhaps he too was afraid of opening himself up because he'd been hurt in the past, but he had so much to offer, and deserved more than being a slave to his job.

'We can keep going, bringing more height to it, but that means thinning the walls more and risking collapse.'

'No, I think I'll quit while I'm ahead.'

She handed him the cutting wire. 'Slide this under, keeping it taut.'

With one swift movement he brought the pot to the edge of the wheel and Evie gently lifted it onto a board to dry.

'It's a little on the wobbly side,' he mused,

head tilted to one side as he studied his creation.

'Rustic, we call it. It's handmade, not moulded in a factory, so it's going to be unique.'

'Very diplomatic.' He grinned. 'I can see why you'd make a good teacher.'

Evie blushed at the praise. 'I'll put it with all my other students' work, ready for firing. Maybe you can come back in and glaze it yourself before the second firing.'

'I'd like that,' he said with a smile which made her blush all over again.

'I should really get on with some work…' She might have managed to distract her thoughts from her poor dog, but now she needed a new diversion away from this man who made her feel things she hadn't felt in a very long time.

'Of course. Maybe I can help with cleaning up or something that'll keep me out of your way.'

Evie directed him towards the dirty utensils at the sink and left him to wash up whilst she set about throwing some plates and pots for firing later. They settled into a busy, quiet contentment. Every now and then she became aware of him watching her, but tried not to let it affect her concentration lest she lose any work.

As the light outside grew dim in the late afternoon her phone rang, and sparked both of them into high alert. Bile rose in her throat, knowing that she might hear some news she wasn't ready for. Jake rinsed his hands and dried them, before lifting her phone from the counter and handing it to her as though he knew it was the only way she was going to answer it.

'Hello?' It wasn't only her voice shaking, her entire body trembling with fear.

Jake came and wrapped his arm around her shoulder, centring her just as he'd done with the clay. As long as she had him to support her, the news would be easier to take.

'Hi, it's Jan here at the surgery. I just wanted you to know that everything went well. Dave came through his operation well and is sleeping off the anaesthetic. We want to keep him in overnight for observation, but you should be able to come and pick him up in the morning.'

Evie managed to mumble her thanks and hang up before bursting into sobs of relief. Jake folded her into his arms and she cried into his chest.

'Your clothes are going to be absolutely ruined,' she managed to joke through the tears.

'I don't care. Do I take it Dave is okay?'

In her relief she'd forgotten to share the good news.

'Yes. Sorry. They're keeping him in overnight and I can collect him in the morning.'

'I'm so pleased for you, Evie.'

He rested his chin on the top of her head and held her tight. They rocked together with the soft strains of the radio playing in the background, like the slow set at the end of a wedding disco, clinging to one another, not wanting it to end. She was drawing too much comfort from his warmth, his strength, and his understanding.

'Thank you so much for staying with me.'

She reluctantly pulled her face away from his chest to look up at him, but neither eased up on the hug, as though they both still needed that contact and letting go would move them on from a place they weren't ready to leave just yet.

'You're welcome.' Jake sounded as choked-up as she was by the whole situation.

For a few moments they simply gazed at one another, and she knew he was thinking about the next move as much as she was. Eventually, they both seemed to come to the inevitable conclusion at the same time. She tilted her face up to meet Jake's as he dipped his head towards her.

The kiss when it came was as sweet and tender as it was passionate. A voice in the distance was telling her to put a stop to this now, that she was vulnerable and not in the right headspace to make rational decisions. Probably why she had no intention of stopping. She was enjoying it too much. Evie reached up and wrapped her arms around his neck, pulling him down further into the kiss. His lips were soft, meshing perfectly with hers, and his teasing tongue drew a satisfied sigh from deep within her.

She needed this moment of happiness. To feel wanted and cherished. There'd be time later for recriminations and regret, but for now she would relish every second of this. Because she'd wanted it since the last time he'd kissed her. After spending the day shopping together, enjoying the market, and killing time waiting for news from the vet, this had seemed inevitable. It was clear they liked each other. There was an attraction they'd given into twice now. Perhaps it was about time she started thinking about dating again.

Specifically, Jake, if he was agreeable. He certainly seemed to be, and they couldn't keep kissing each other and pretending it hadn't happened. That would tear her up as much as if he deliberately hurt her like Bailey. Maybe, just maybe, she was ready to take the risk of being with someone again when this felt so much better than being on her own.

Her phone rang, the outside world bleeding into their little haven and making them face reality. One in which they weren't a couple, and shouldn't be doing this.

'You should get that.' Jake stepped back, setting her free from his embrace, and she could already sense the shutters coming down again.

If she wasn't afraid that it might be the vet getting in touch to say something had happened to Dave, she might have let it ring out. Instead, she left Jake so she could answer it. When she saw it was Ursula's number on the screen she swore inwardly that her friend had interrupted the moment. Then immediately felt bad because she knew Ursula was only phoning out of concern.

'Hey, Ursula.'

'How is he? How are you? I'm so sorry. I only took my eyes off him for a second when the postman came and he slipped right out past us. He can move quick when he wants to.' Her words spilled out on top of each other until she burst into loud tears on the other end of the phone.

'He's fine, Ursula. I'm okay too. Honestly. It's no one's fault.'

Out of the corner of her eye, Evie could see Jake take off his apron and put his jacket back on. He was getting ready to run.

She waved at him to stay put.

'I've been so worried about you both. I wouldn't blame you if you sack me for gross incompetence or something.' Her friend's melodrama made her smile. At least she wasn't the only one prone to sentimentality over a dog. Or catastrophising.

'I'm not going to sack you, Ursula…'

Jake opened the door and she frowned at him, hoping to portray a look which said *Don't you dare go anywhere*. Apparently, it didn't have the desired effect as he gestured towards his watch and shrugged.

Ursula was rambling on about making every cup of tea in the studio until the end of time if Evie forgave her. Something she would hold her to, but wasn't the most pressing thing on her mind at the minute.

'Ursula, I'm going to have to go. I'll call you later.' She hung up. 'Where do you think you're going?'

'I have to get back to work. I'm glad everything's okay.' He had the audacity to actually walk away, but Evie followed him into the corridor.

'We're not actually going to discuss the fact that we keep kissing each other?'

Jake hung his head. 'I'm sorry. It's an emotional time, but I don't think it's a good idea for either of us to take things any further. I can't be the man you need, and to promise you any different would be a lie.'

With that, he turned on his heel and walked away, Not even giving her the chance to put up an argument. To tell him she didn't need promises of for ever. That for now she was content to be reminded that she was wanted. He was in too much of a hurry to get away to hear a word of it.

Something told her it was the last she'd see of him until the wedding. If he even still wanted her there.

CHAPTER SEVEN

'HAVE I TOLD you that you look beautiful?' Jake whispered to Evie as they sat waiting for the bride to appear.

'Yes. Several times.' She blushed in that adorable way that made him think people hadn't told her that enough.

'Well, you do.'

'Thank you. You look good too. I like your tie.' She nodded towards the coordinated tie she'd bought him when they'd gone clothes shopping together.

The conversation the whole way to the register office had been the same. Awkward. Stilted. Making it feel as though they'd never shared anything other than a car here. He knew that was his fault. Since that afternoon in her studio, he'd cooled things off between them. To the point he was surprised she'd even agreed to still come to the wedding. Perhaps she'd only done so out of misplaced guilt over the outfit he'd bought. Either way, he was lucky Evie was still speaking to him.

It seemed the more he enjoyed spending time with Evie, the more he freaked out over it. Having the whole day together, investing in the welfare of her dog, not to mention kissing her again, had taken him to a place he wasn't ready to be in. He'd felt like part of a couple, waiting for news about her dog. Shared her happiness and relief when everything had turned out okay, and let himself give in to the temptation to take her in his arms again. All of which would've been perfectly normal to anyone else, but to someone who knew not to get close to anyone it spelled disaster.

He didn't want to hurt Evie by leading her on when nothing could come of it. Settling down wasn't on the cards for him, and it was clear that was what she wanted in a partner. When today was over it was probably best to make a clean break so neither of them got caught up in this fantasy of being a real couple.

The lilting music from the harpist at the front of the room marked the bride's entrance, along with the creaking of chairs as everyone turned to take a look. Jake didn't. It felt weird being here to witness his mother getting married to someone he barely knew. Gary, his soon-to-be stepfather, was just one in a long line of boyfriends in his mother's quest for love. The difference being that this one was prepared to make a public commitment. Not that Jake thought it would last. It never did.

'You look like your mum,' Evie whispered.

She apparently had opted to sneak a peek at the bridal party currently making its way down the aisle.

'Yeah,' Jake mumbled, hoping it was sufficient.

Now that this was really happening, he was beginning to feel that familiar tensing in his body. As though he was the only one who could see disaster coming and no one else would listen. Instead, he was supposed to sit and smile and agree with how romantic it all was, knowing it was a car crash waiting to happen. And that was before his dad even made an appearance. Something else he wasn't looking forward to.

He drew some comfort from the fact Evie was here with him. Despite all the ways he'd messed things up, she was still supporting him. Maybe if he'd had someone willing to do that earlier in his life, he wouldn't be so reticent about being with anyone now.

His mother and sister were level with him now. Donna managed a sly wave to him and Evie and he knew she was busting to speak to his plus-one.

The nervous groom, who couldn't have been more than ten years older than Jake, turned to meet his bride, the romantic moment somewhat sullied by the sound of Jake's father sighing and checking his watch, letting everyone know he had better places to be and giving every appearance that he was so busy they were lucky he'd made time to come at all. Anyone else might have wondered why his mum had invited her ex at all, except for Jake, who suspected she still held a candle for him. Both of his parents were lost causes. And the very example of how relationships went wrong.

He nudged Evie and nodded towards the end of the aisle opposite. 'That's my dad.'

She leaned around him to see for herself. 'Huh. He doesn't seem so scary.'

That right there was the reason he'd brought her here today. Whether it was showing him it was fun to get his work suit covered in clay or reminding him that his father was human, Evie had a way of bringing him back down to earth.

Jake zoned out as the vows went on. They were nonsense anyway. In his experience, they were empty promises, impossible for a couple to keep. No one knew for certain what the future held and vowing to stay together for ever seemed naïve at best, and a lie at worst. If sickness or poverty became an issue they couldn't weather together, or one half of the partnership didn't want to settle down in one place, it wasn't a realistic notion. Which was why Jake didn't believe in marriage. It was the ultimate commitment and, as far as he could tell, the ultimate heartbreak waiting to happen. That was why he was happier being single, and free from expectations and responsibility. Wasn't he?

He glanced at Evie sitting beside him, already dabbing at her eyes, truly caught up in the romance already, thoughts of their day together running through his head like a movie montage. Sharing a hot chocolate together, Evie showing him how to throw a pot, hugging when Dave got the all-clear, and kissing when temptation proved too much. Had he really been happier these past days without her than those few hours he'd spent in her company? Not according to Donna, who'd likened him to a bear with a sore head lately.

It begged the question: what was so bad about the idea of getting more involved with her than he already was? Okay, so things might not work out. 'For ever' was not always a possibility. But was she worth at least opening his heart up to the idea of something more than her being his fake date?

As his mother said 'I do' and exchanged rings with her new husband, Jake realised he only had today to decide what he was going to do. If he was prepared to let her walk out of his life for good in just a matter of hours. After the reception she was under no obligation to him so he had to make that decision that might just go against everything he'd been telling himself about relationships for years.

Not an easy task against the backdrop of his parents and the dysfunctional relationships at play here today. He only hoped there was a pivotal moment which would help him take that leap of faith because, deep down, he knew he didn't want to lose Evie for good.

The whole day was overwhelming for Evie. She'd never felt so welcome and included as she did by Jake's family and friends, who all appeared delighted she was there. It was difficult to get used to when she'd spent her teen-age years being treated as an inconvenience.

Jake seemed just as uncomfortable with the attention, though for different reasons. She was beginning to wonder why he'd invited her at all when he'd been so reluctant to introduce her to people, or talk about their 'relationship'. He might as well have come on his own if he didn't want people to believe they were together.

They'd got caught up at the register office for a while as guests rushed to meet his 'girl-friend'. At one point she'd thought they were getting more attention than the bride and groom. They'd both protested when the photographer had asked her to be in the family group photos, but his mother and sister had insisted. Something they might come to regret when they saw the dark expression he'd been wearing in most of them.

As she shuffled away from intruding further upon the wedding party she had absolutely nothing to do with, Donna grabbed her by the arm.

'I can't tell you how happy I am to see you with my big brother. He's been so grumpy these past days, even more so than usual. I was worried you'd broken up already.'

Evie smiled politely. 'I'm Evie. It's nice to meet you.'

'Donna. You have no idea what a big deal it is for him to bring someone with him to this sort of thing. I hope I get to talk to you more at the reception.'

'I don't know if I'm going…' The way she was feeling at the minute it seemed like a pointless exercise if it was just going to make her and Jake even more uncomfortable.

'Of course you are. You're practically family now.' Donna gave her a wink before she walked away, just in time for Jake to catch the end of the conversation.

'We should probably head on to the hotel for the reception now.'

Evie didn't think it was possible for Jake to look even more disturbed by today's events but she'd been wrong. As if she'd gatecrashed the wedding and announced herself as the next Mrs Hanley.

She managed to hold her tongue as she tee-tered over to the car behind him, struggling to keep up with his long deliberate strides in the heels she wasn't used to wearing. It was only when they were safely ensconced away from everyone else, the atmosphere tense and

uneasy, that she said her piece. At this point
there was nothing to lose.

'I'm not going.'

'Pardon?'

'To the reception. I'm not going. So you
may as well drop me back home.' She put her
seatbelt on and sat, hands in her lap, ready for
him to drive.

'But the deal…'

'I came as your plus-one. Say I'm sick or
something. I'm sure no one will notice.' It was
a lie. Donna was sure to have a hundred questions about why she hadn't accompanied him
to the reception dinner, but that would be for
Jake to explain. It wasn't Evie's problem any
more.

He still hadn't started the car and she was
stuck here until he did.

'But I need you there.'

She looked at him in disbelief, surprised
to find an anxious face looking back at her.

'Why? So you can take your bad mood out
on me, Jake? You've made it clear you don't
want me here. It's like you're embarrassed to
be seen with me.'

'Never.'

His insistence didn't erase his attitude the

whole time his family and friends had stopped to talk to them.

'I don't know why you wanted me to come if you didn't want people to think we're together. I don't understand you, Jake. What I do know, though, is that I don't have to be a part of whatever is going on with you. I've had a lifetime of feeling as though I'm not wanted. That I don't fit in. I don't need that in my life any more. Especially with someone who's not going to be around after tonight. I'd rather cut my losses now. Thank you for being there when I needed you but I'm sorry, I have to put my own feelings first for a change.'

It was kind of cathartic to actually say what was on her mind for once. A speech she'd often rehearsed saying to her family but had never had the courage to voice in person. Ironic that it was Jake who'd probably given her the confidence and safe space to do so. Weirdly, she was confident enough around him to say how she was feeling.

'I'm sorry. You're right. You don't deserve any of this.' He started the car, but Evie still wanted an explanation.

'Then tell me what's going on, Jake.' She reached across his lap and turned the key, switching the ignition back off.

'I thought by having someone with me it would stop the judgement. Then everyone would stop quizzing me about why I don't have a partner, like I'm some freak of nature. I didn't expect you to have this impact. Everyone's so happy for me. But none of it is real.' His hands were still gripping the steering wheel as he spoke.

'But this was what you wanted.' It was so confusing to her. Goodness knew what was going on in his head.

He finally let go of the wheel, letting the circulation back, his knuckles no longer a deathly white. 'I know, I know. I guess it's just opened my eyes to how different things might have been. If my unstable childhood hadn't had such an effect on me, perhaps I would've settled down with someone. I could've been happy.'

'And you're not?' Evie would've imagined someone in his position, with money and a successful business, was content with his lot, but Jake certainly didn't sound happy.

'I thought I was, but now I'm wondering what I'm missing out on. My parents splitting up, my breakup with my ex…all confirmed that relationships don't last. They're just painful. I told myself I didn't need anyone else in my life who could hurt me in the future. Then I stumbled into your studio.' He gave her a lopsided smile, reminding her of that bemused stranger that night who'd listened to her strange tale of needing a fake date to impress her family and agreed to do it for her.

Though she didn't know how she'd changed his view of relationships when she was just as afraid of being in one. On that account they were on the same page. Long-term commitment meant heartache down the line.

'I haven't asked you for anything, Jake. Nor do I have any expectations beyond tonight, or even this minute. I came because I owed you a favour, and okay, yes, I like you. I don't think we'd keep kissing each other if the feeling wasn't mutual. But I'm not looking for anything more, if that's what you're worried about. Bailey hurt me too much to consider another relationship. If, however, you still want me to accompany you to the reception—'

'I do.'

'If you promise not to be moody—'

'I do.'

It was beginning to sound as though they were making their own vows. Ironic, when he wanted the opposite to 'till death us do part' where she was concerned.

'Then I will go with you. On the proviso that we just go and have a good time, and forget all this other stuff you're currently over-thinking.'

Evie knew she was asking a lot, but she didn't want to spend the rest of the night regretting not walking away now. He'd made it clear he wasn't interested in pursuing anything with her, so she needed to put all thoughts of it out of her head too. If this was the last time they were going to be together she simply wanted them to enjoy it, so she'd have a memory to look back on fondly. A nicer one than his blatant unease at people thinking they were a real couple.

'Done. I'm sorry that I made you feel uncomfortable. That's totally on me. I'm the one out of my depth pretending to be part of a couple. It was easier doing it at your home, with people who didn't know me beyond anything we told them was the truth. This is a deception involving my parents and my sister I probably should have thought over a bit more.'

'I'm beginning to think that myself,' Evie joked, well aware they couldn't go back and change things now. They simply had to press on as well as they could, and hope for the best.

At least lying, and the consequences of it, weren't something he did easily. Jake had a conscience. Unlike Bailey, who'd lied and cheated on her for months without a second thought of what it would do to her. Evie was sure that part of what was troubling him was how upset everyone would be once they found out the truth. Something she selfishly hoped would never come to light, so they wouldn't think badly of her either.

'So, we're going?' He was leaving the final decision down to her, then she only had herself to blame when she was left bereft at the end of the night, knowing she'd never see Jake again.

'Y-e-s.' She said it slowly, almost questioning her own answer. As well as her sanity.

Jake was mindful of Evie every time someone approached them to say hello. He didn't want her to end up resenting him for bringing her here, so he was doing his best to be sociable. Something that didn't come easy to him when he was used to doing only things he wanted, with only his own feelings to take into consideration. He supposed that was a selfish kind of way to live, but it was how he'd protected himself all these years. It was only Evie being so honest and upfront about how his actions were making her uncomfortable which made him take a hard look at himself. Perhaps there had been a transition in him at some point where he'd changed from the wounded party into the transgressor, and the thought didn't sit easily with him.

Other than his sister, Evie was the first person to hold a mirror up and ask him to look at his behaviour. He didn't want to be someone else in her life making her miserable or feeling as though she was somehow inferior, because it wasn't true. Nor was he happy to make anyone else feel that way. Whatever his personal feelings surrounding the day, or the people he interacted with, he was determined to play nice. Otherwise, they were all going to wonder why the hell someone as lovely as Evie would ever want to be with him.

'Hello, son.' The appearance of his father in the hotel lobby as they reached the reception venue was going to be a serious test of his new vow.

'Dad.' There was an awkward few seconds' silence as the three of them stood staring at one another, sipping the complimentary glasses of Buck's Fizz they'd been handed on arrival, whilst the rest of the guests mingled and chattered around them.

It was Evie who broke the silence and held out her hand. 'I'm Evie. It's nice to meet you.'

'John Hanley. So, are you two together then?' As expected, he got straight to the point, not wasting time on small talk.

Evie took a strategic sip of her drink, leaving him to answer that one.

'Yes.' He could be equally efficient with his words.

'Hello, Father dear. Talking the ear off our latest member of the family, are we?' Donna appeared and rescued them all, as she kissed their father on the cheek.

They'd always had a better relationship than Jake and his father had ever had. Most likely because she'd still been young when their parents had split up, hadn't experienced his absence, or moved around as much. Growing up with their mother, in a settled home, had been a much calmer experience and Donna had obviously benefitted from it. Jake mused that the emotional, and perhaps psychological, damage of his father's behaviour had already been done to him by then.

'Hi, sis. You look amazing.' Jake gave her a quick hug, pleased to see her more than ever.

'I know, but look at you two. Twit-twoo. And Dad, you're immaculate, as always.'

She looked them all up and down, and Jake knew he should take a leaf out of his little sister's book when it came to successful mingling. Always ready with a compliment and ease of conversation, she was always the most popular person in the room. Though he reminded himself that her openness came at a cost too. She was the one who got her heart broken over and over again, a glutton for punishment when it came to love, but as she'd told Jake, she'd never give up trying to find the right 'one'. He admired her tenacity, even if she shared their mother's fatal flaw of romanticising life. One thing his father had taught him was that it was tough and not something you simply floated through. You had to make a path for yourself and not wait for life to happen to you.

'You have to make an effort, don't you?' Jake's father straightened his perfect tie.

He always dressed smart. Shoes shined, trousers freshly pressed and not a hair out of place. Jake supposed that was something else he'd had ingrained in him. Perhaps that was why he'd enjoyed that day at Evie's studio. There was something liberating about getting clay on his clothes, an act of rebellion in a way. She'd shown him he didn't always have to be immaculately turned out, and it didn't matter if he wasn't. The world hadn't ended because he'd got a bit dirty.

Evie helped him relax. He wasn't the tightly wound ball of stress he usually was around her. That was probably why he'd wanted her here with him in what he knew was going to be one of those stress-filled situations. Though all he'd managed to do so far was instil that sense of anxiety-induced propriety that he'd grown up with. Hopefully, a few drinks and dancing would help them both relax a bit more.

'I'm afraid it's a bit of a waste of time in my line of work. That's why it's nice for me to have a chance to dress up for once.' Evie joined in the conversation, though he knew it would spark more interest from his sister.

He was right.

'What do you do for a living, Evie?'

'Ceramics. I have my own studio, and I run some pottery classes.'

Donna's mouth dropped open and she stared at Jake. 'You dark horse.'

'Yes, Evie runs the pottery nights you told me to enquire about,' he conceded.

'So you booked Evie for the team bonding, then you asked her out for some one-on-one bonding?' his sister teased, mischief in her eyes as she watched him over the rim of her glass, waiting for a reaction.

'Not exactly. As I recall, you didn't actually book anything.' Now Evie was getting in on the act, making him look bad.

'I must've been distracted...' He reminded her that she was having some sort of existential crisis when he'd walked in and hoped that would be enough to end that particular topic of conversation.

'Well, you might have solved the issue of your desolate love life, but you still have to sort something out for your employees. He needs to work on his personal skills on more than just the tutor.' Donna was openly laughing now, and Jake couldn't help but smile.

He'd definitely taken her advice when it came to being more accessible, but only when it came to Evie. Even then he had a tendency to blast her with that cold front when it felt as though she was breaching his defences.

'I'll arrange something. Don't worry.' There was still time, although things were bound to be booking up this close to Christmas. Perhaps they'd have to take a look at a New Year's get-together instead.

'I still have room in my schedule. I could put something in the diary if you want to book a session?'

Now Evie was putting him on the spot he was having to think about whether or not he wanted to make another arrangement to see her again. Although the answer was a definite yes, he still had to question if it was a good idea. Though he didn't think *I'm afraid I'll like her too much* was going to be a suitable excuse to his sister if he had to explain why he hadn't booked after all.

'Sure. I assume you'll be there too, sis?'

'With bells on. I am not going to miss you up to your elbows in clay, swearing when the wheel fights back.'

'As a matter of fact, Jake's quite a dab hand at throwing.' It didn't matter that Evie was bigging him up when he saw the dark look on his father's face.

'Sounds like a waste of time to me,' he grumbled.

Evie's stricken look was reminiscent of that evening at her family home when she'd been the object of unfair criticism there too. Jake immediately felt that same need to protect her.

'Sometimes you need a bit of fun in your life, Dad. And actually, Evie is a very skilled ceramicist as well as a tutor. So I'd appreciate it if you respected that.'

There was something liberating in speaking his mind instead of keeping it bottled up. He could see why Evie had let loose on him earlier. It was possible if he'd been so bold when he was younger that the dynamic between him and his father might've been different now. It was that overwhelming need to defend Evie that had finally prompted him into action now. She was changing his staid life in so many ways it should've been scary for someone so reluctant to change. However, Jake was finding each small concession to his usual composure refreshing. Mind-blowing. A relief.

'I, for one, am looking forward to your class, Evie. Now, I suppose we should go in and find our seats for the meal.' Donna changed the subject quickly and motioned towards the rest of the guests, who were filtering into the dining room. She'd always been the one to defuse any tension when it came to Jake and his dad. Some things never changed.

'I'm at the top table, but I'll catch up with you later,' Donna promised with another round of cheek kisses before disappearing into the room in a swirl of chiffon.

'It looks like I've been stuck at the table with the distant cousins and barely known acquaintances.' His father bemoaned his lot, though Jake hadn't expected him to stay beyond the ceremony. Perhaps his mother hadn't either and that was why she'd seated him at one of the far tables.

'Why wouldn't your mother sit you together?' Evie enquired as his father went looking for his seat. Jake wouldn't put it past him to try and swap with someone else in a more prominent position.

'She knows better. Probably trying to avoid any sort of scene. Also, I think she originally wanted me at the top table. She asked me to give her away, but it wasn't something I was keen to do.'

He didn't want to be a part of something he didn't believe in, but he'd agreed to attend once he'd known Evie would be coming with him. That concession had kept everyone happy. Though he hadn't expected the idea of bringing a plus-one to cause so much excitement in the family.

'How did she take that?'

Jake shrugged. 'As well as could be expected, but she knows I'm not into the whole marriage idea. Bringing you was the sweetener.'

'Ah, I see. Well, at least we're sitting together.'

She took his hand and he let her lead him to the table closest to his mother and her new groom. Far enough away from his father that he didn't have to be on guard, waiting for him to insult Evie again, forcing him to react. At least now they might be able to do some of that relaxing and having fun she'd talked about.

The dinner and speeches had gone well, although Evie hadn't eaten much of her meal, nerves getting the better of her. She already felt out of place and it hadn't helped when Jake's father had looked down his nose at her choice of career. The only reason that she hadn't let it get to her too much was the fact that Jake had stood up for her. Again.

She knew she shouldn't rely on him to ride in and save her every time she was in distress, but it was nice to have someone there willing to do so. In contrast, his sister Donna seemed lovely, and very friendly. Though Jake had warned her that his mum and sister were keen to have him paired off and in their heads they were probably already making plans for their nuptials, making her wonder even more why he'd gone ahead with this.

It had taken a lot of courage for her to speak out in the car back at the register office, but it had needed to be said. For her peace of mind, if nothing else.

'Sorry I haven't got talking to you before now, Evie. I don't remember being this in demand on my first wedding day.' Jake's mother came to join them at their table once the hotel was getting things ready for the evening entertainment and an influx of new guests who hadn't been lucky enough to get an invite to the actual ceremony.

'That's okay. It's your big day. You and Donna look beautiful.'

It was easy to compliment her when she was glowing. The elegant bride, who Evie estimated to be in her early sixties, was wearing a tasteful ivory lace dress with a faux fur cape, and looked every bit as happy as she hoped to be some day.

'Thank you. So do you. Now I know who's

behind the change in my son recently.' She gave an embarrassed Jake a shoulder squeeze.

'I don't know about that.'

Now it was Evie's turn to squirm. She didn't want to take any credit for anything Jake-related when she was nothing more than his fake date. After tonight she wasn't going to be anything to him. Unless he wanted her to, in which case she'd left the door open for him with the whole pottery class setup.

'You got him to come here, so I'm grateful for that. Now, I have a whole floor of rooms reserved for family. I hope you're staying the night.'

Before Evie was forced to make some feeble excuse to his mother, Jake stepped in.

'I'm afraid not. I'm driving Evie back so I won't be drinking. I don't need a room.'

Evie supposed that was mainly who they were for—guests who partook of a little too much alcohol over the course of the day's celebrations. She knew Jake couldn't wait to get away so would be leaving as soon as he'd done his bit here as the dutiful son.

'Well, the room is there should you want it. Evie can always get a taxi if she needs to. Right, I must get back to my new husband. Do try to get to know Gary, son. I promise he's not like all the others. Save a dance for me.' She kissed her fingers and touched Jake's cheek, a gesture Evie was sure wasn't a one-off. He didn't seem the type to go in for public displays of affection and she wondered if this was his mother's only way of getting to express her love for him.

Once again, Evie felt a surge of love and empathy for the young Jake, who perhaps hadn't been used to a tactile family. His father certainly didn't seem the type to go in for kisses and cuddles, much like her stepmother.

Perhaps they were both victims of their dysfunctional families and damaged relationships, but they were old enough to make a change themselves. Break that pattern.

It could be that started with a simple thing like dating again. She didn't know how Jake would feel about that, but she was beginning to think she was ready to dip a toe back into that pool at least.

'Your mum's right. I can get a taxi if you want to stay here tonight. It's her wedding day, you should be celebrating with her.'

Evie didn't want to stand in the way of him making any progress where his family were concerned. Both Donna and his mum had commented on his improved mood, and the fact that he'd agreed to come here at all seemed to be heralding some sort of emotional change. It could be down to the time he'd spent with her family, and realised his wasn't all that bad in comparison. Or he'd realised how lucky he was to have people who genuinely loved him. Whatever was drawing him closer to them, she didn't want to throw a spanner in the works now and interrupt any progress.

'I might have a couple of drinks. I'll probably need them. We can still get a taxi. I know you're off the clock come midnight.'

'Midnight? That's pushing it. I think you only managed a few hours in my family's company before we did a disappearing act.'

Evie liked to needle him every now and then to keep things light. Sometimes Jake needed reminding that not everything had to be serious. After meeting his father, it wasn't surprising.

'You know you're free to go any time, Evie. I'm not holding you hostage.'

She gathered up her bag and pretended to leave. 'In that case…'

Jake reached out and grabbed her wrist, a genuine look of panic in his wide eyes. 'Please don't go. I need you.'

Evie plonked back down in her seat, her knees weak and her heart sore for him that he worried so much about being left alone. No doubt a throwback to his childhood, when he'd been forced to follow his father's military career around the world, never having a stable home environment.

'I was only joking.' She took his hand across the table. 'I'll see you through whatever happens tonight.'

After that, she wasn't sure. It was down to Jake to decide if he was willing to venture into anything more than a fake relationship with her.

He gave her hand a quick squeeze then got to his feet. 'I think I'll go and see about those drinks.'

She watched him up at the bar whilst she made small talk with the friends of the groom they'd been seated with during dinner. Jake was drawing admiring glances from a lot of people in the room, not that he seemed to notice. As he stood at the bar waiting for their drinks, he was approached by a couple of women he seemed to know as he hugged them on sight. He was smiling and nodding, engaged in conversation, and appeared to be enjoying this interaction, as opposed to any he'd had with his family so far. Even more than he had with her.

She couldn't take her eyes off what was happening, a burning sensation rising inside her that she recognised as jealousy. The absurdity of feeling territorial over a man who was uncomfortable with her as his fake date made her either want to laugh or weep. Later, in the privacy of her own empty home, she might indulge in both. Because it was becoming increasingly apparent that she didn't just want to try dating again. There was only one man she wanted to try it with. Jake.

When he started walking back towards her, drinks in hand, smile on his face, she was almost giddy with the anticipation of him coming back to her. She hated herself. Fan-girling certainly wasn't the way to convince Jake that she was the girl for him. Nor was it the way to break herself back into dating if she was hanging on his every word and every second of attention that he afforded her.

She needed to slow this down, and take it one moment at a time. Otherwise, she was going to have her heart broken even sooner than expected. One minute past midnight, by all accounts. Unless something drastic happened between now and then, Cinderella would be going home in her pumpkin carriage and leaving the handsome prince behind for ever.

'A glass of wine for the lady.' He delivered her drink with a flourish, his mood clearly buoyed by his interaction at the bar.

Evie seethed.

'Thank you.' She bit her lip to prevent herself from saying anything else which would give away her irrational jealousy and raise all manner of red flags to him.

He sat down, still smiling about something. 'I ran into a couple of cousins I haven't seen in years. I actually forgot I have family beyond Donna and my parents because we see them so rarely.'

'That must've been so nice for you.' Captain Green Eyes was able to stand down.

'You know, it's easy to see all the negatives of family when you haven't had a particularly happy childhood. It's funny how something like this can reconnect you with some of the positives you've forgotten about.'

'Oh?'

Unfortunately, Evie couldn't relate when June and Courtney were the only family she had, and any good memories had died along with her father.

'They reminded me that I used to go to the under-eighteen discos with them when we were kids. Apparently, they have photographic evidence of my boyband haircut and penchant for skinny jeans. They were complimenting my improved taste in clothes.'

He shook his head, but Evie could see he was genuinely pleased to have reconnected with this part of his past. It could only be good for his future relations with his family. Perhaps he might look to cultivate more of a relationship with these cousins and have a more rounded view, not only of his family and relationships in general but also himself.

'I'm so going to need a copy of those photographs or, you know, at least see them.'

It dawned on her it would be weird to want photographs of a man she wasn't supposed to care about, or see again.

'I'm not sure anyone needs to see those...'

'Well, I'm sure it was good to see your cousins again.'

'It was. It really was.' Jake really seemed to be relaxing, becoming more open to the idea of being with family.

Evie wondered if he still needed her at all, but the truth was she was reluctant to leave anyway. She wasn't ready to walk away from him and the feelings he was reawakening in her. Jake Hanley was making her realise that her life hadn't ended when Bailey had cheated on her. The problem now was what to do about it.

CHAPTER EIGHT

JAKE DIDN'T KNOW if it was down to the alcohol, the fact that his father had left the venue or that he had Evie with him, but he was beginning to enjoy the evening. The pressure was off now that the wedding was over, the family had met Evie, and got over the novelty of him bringing a woman with him. They'd simply accepted her, and them as a couple. And why wouldn't they? Evie was amazing, and they made a good team. She'd be the perfect partner if he was ever ready to have one. But he wasn't. That didn't mean he wanted to say goodbye though. He just wished there were a happy medium somewhere so he wasn't under the pressure of expectations or commitment.

'Are you going to sit there brooding all night, big brother, or are you going to loosen that tie and come and dance?' Donna, who had been up on the floor boogying with the rest of the bridal party, grabbed his hand and pulled him from his seat.

'You know I can't dance,' he protested, shooting Evie an apologetic look for leaving her.

'You *don't* dance. There's a difference. Besides, it's the only chance I'll have to quiz you on Evie.' Donna twirled herself around his fingertips, forcing him into being her dance partner.

He knew it would be futile to try and avoid her questions. All he could hope for was that this song would end soon, along with his humiliation.

'What do you want to know?'

'Why you've been hiding her.'

'I haven't been hiding her. I simply haven't let you know about her. There's a difference.' He felt smug about using her quote against her until she pulled him into hold and made him dance with her.

'What's so bad about her, or me, that you couldn't tell me?'

'Nothing. It's called a private life, Donna. This is exactly why I didn't tell you about Evie. So you and Mum didn't get carried away and make a big deal out of it.'

'But it is a big deal. I can see she makes

you happy, and that's all we want for you. Is that so bad?'

'I guess not.' He felt like a heel now, projecting his fears onto her. It was his idea to let people think they were together, so he shouldn't be surprised when they asked questions. Seeing him with a woman was unusual, so the fact that he'd even brought her to the wedding could easily be mistaken as a relationship.

'You don't want to let her slip through your fingers, so why don't you give her a good time, and show her what you're capable of?' Donna spun herself out of his arms and grabbed hold of Evie, placing her hand in Jake's, before going to find herself a new dance partner.

He knew she was talking about dancing, but her words applied to other areas of his life where he held back. Like loving someone, sharing his life and imagining a future with them.

'Sorry about this,' he mumbled into Evie's ear, knowing it was going to look odd if they didn't have at least one dance together now they were both on the floor.

'It's fine. I love to dance. I just don't get the opportunity to do it much.'

'You had lessons too?'

'Nothing as glamorous as that. I just used to dance in my room when I was younger. It was my outlet. Wait… You took lessons? You actually know how to dance?' Her eyes were wide with surprise, and perhaps something bordering on admiration.

Talk about giving himself away.

'Yeah. Mum insisted on it. She said a man needed to know how to dance if he wanted to impress a lady. Poor Mum thought everyone was a romantic like her.'

'No, she's right. I'm very impressed.'

'I haven't even showed you my best moves yet.' He couldn't resist the chance to deploy his secret weapon just this one time and perhaps give Evie a sample of his skills. Even if he was a bit rusty.

As the music changed to a slower tempo, more suitable for ballroom dancing, he switched up from gently swaying together and took Evie into close position, increasing their body contact with his right hand at her back, forcing her to wrap one hand around his neck as he clasped the other in his free hand.

'But I don't know how to dance.' The panic was there in her eyes as well as her voice that she'd make a fool of herself, but Jake wouldn't let that happen.

'It's okay. I'll lead.' The steps came flooding back to him and she let him sweep her around the floor, eventually relaxing, a smile on her face as they spun around.

He'd forgotten how much he actually enjoyed dancing. His rebellion against it mostly born of his mother's insistence that he needed to learn to impress anyone. Now he was glad he was able to show off a little for Evie. He was probably holding her a little closer than usually permitted, holding eye contact when he shouldn't, because he wanted to enjoy her reaction. And he certainly shouldn't be feeling the way he was with her in his arms. Something that felt more intimate than those passionate kisses they kept indulging in.

He was sorry when the music stopped.

'I… I think I need some air.' Evie was barely out of his arms before she was running off the dance floor, leaving him staring after her, bewildered.

Jake had no idea what was wrong when she'd seemed so happy dancing with him only moments ago. What he did know was that he cared enough about her to find out and went after her, out through the doors and into the wintry night.

'Evie?' He found her in the little thatched

summer house which, with its open front, provided no protection from the icy air.

Her features illuminated by the festive lights strung around the roof and heather-clad walls, she looked like a Christmas fairy sitting on the little bench inside.

'Sorry. I just needed to get some fresh air,' she said, moving up to make room for him.

'I think you've had a little too much. You're shivering.'

Without her pashmina she was bound to be feeling the cold. Jake took off his jacket and hung it around her shoulders.

'Do you want me to go?' He didn't want to impose if she needed some time out. As long as he knew she was okay, and not about to freeze to death, he'd leave her alone if she needed some space.

'No. Stay.' She reached out her hand and placed it on his leg.

Enough contact to send all his nerve-endings into overdrive, the warmth of her hand resting on his thigh creating urges inside him it was becoming increasingly difficult to ignore.

'What's wrong, Evie? Was it the dancing? My family?'

He wanted her to tell him so he could fix it

and make things better for her. It was obvious there was something bothering her. He just hoped it wasn't down to him, because he'd hate himself if he'd upset her when she'd done so much for him simply by being here today.

She shook her head and gave him a sad little smile that only made him ache for her more. 'It's me. I shouldn't have come here tonight.'

Uneasiness settled in Jake's stomach at the thought she'd felt pressured to stay. Obviously whilst he'd thought she was enjoying herself, it had all been part of the act she'd agreed to play in front of his family.

'I'm sorry. Do you want me to get you a taxi?' He pulled out his phone, eager to make amends, horrified with himself for not realising sooner that she wasn't comfortable. The fact that he'd been enjoying their turn around the dance floor together only made it worse.

'No. You don't understand.'

'Then tell me,' he begged, her feelings more important to him than he'd ever expected. Something that went far beyond the idea of a fake relationship.

'I don't want to leave. I don't want you to leave. I don't want tonight to end.'

Tear-filled eyes locked onto his and he was

so lost in them for a moment it took a while to register what she was saying.

'That's why you're upset? Because tonight marks the end of our…arrangement?' After the way he'd been feeling, it was a relief to know that was what the problem was. That she liked him, not that she couldn't stomach playing the role of girlfriend for a second longer.

'I know this wasn't part of the deal, and it's not your problem really. Forget I said anything. I'll deal with it. You go back inside and be with your family.'

She was rambling again. It was a habit he recognised now when she was nervous, an adorable quirk that made Evie the woman she was. The woman who was making him question his attitude towards his love life.

For once he decided to act on instinct, and everything in this moment was telling him to kiss her.

When he didn't respond to her confession immediately, Evie started to spiral again. 'You know what? I'll go. Tell everyone I had a migraine or something. I'm sure you can come up with an excuse. I'm sorry for ruining things—'

Jake reached across and planted his lips on hers, kissing her not only to shut her up so he could try and think, but also to remind himself if it was as good as he remembered. It was. So much, in fact, that the idea of rational thought went out of the window. The only important thing in his world right now was tasting her on his tongue again.

He cupped her face in his hands and kissed her thoroughly, taking his time, unlike their previous lapses. As though he could afford the luxury now they'd both given permission for it to happen. It was clear she liked him as much as he'd come to like her. Never more so than when she wrapped her arms around his neck and pressed herself closer. Jake vaguely registered that his jacket had fallen on the ground in the process when he was so acutely aware of her body against his. Although they'd given into temptation before, this was the first time they'd leaned into a kiss. Really explored one another and how they were making each other feel in the moment. He didn't want to think of beyond now, the implications and complications of taking things further. Moving on to somewhere he wasn't sure either of them was ready for.

Despite the heat infusing his body, and the passion in their embrace, Jake could feel her body trembling. He wasn't vain enough to believe it was solely down to him, and realised that the cold was seeping its way into Evie's bones. As much as he was enjoying their time alone, they couldn't stay here for ever.

'We should probably go back inside before you catch pneumonia.' He picked up his jacket and draped it back around her shoulders.

'What happens now?'

'I have no idea,' he said honestly, his smile giving nothing away of the turmoil going on in his head, his body or his heart.

Well, he knew what certain parts of his anatomy wanted to happen, but it was his head that had dictated his actions until recently. Right now, it was fighting with every instinct that told him to take the next step with Evie. Just because he liked her, wanted to be with her, it didn't change anything else in his life. He still didn't want a commitment. Nor did he want to hurt Evie. Yet he had this feeling they could have something special, and it was obvious Evie had the same intuition. Otherwise, they wouldn't be so reluctant for the evening, for this 'fake' relationship, to end.

'We could just let this night pan out and not think about what happens next,' Evie suggested with a twinkle in her eye. It was very tempting, and so was she.

'You mean spend the night together?' The idea had merits but he didn't know what was in it for Evie. She'd already been hurt once and he didn't want her to think they had a future together when he knew it was never going to happen.

'Why not? People do it all the time.' She shrugged nonchalantly but Jake wasn't convinced she had such a casual attitude towards sex when it was clear she hadn't been with anyone since Bailey, her long-term boyfriend.

'But not you.'

'Yeah, well, long-term commitment didn't work out so well. Not for me, at least.'

'So, what? A one-night stand?' Jake wasn't sure that was going to solve any problems for them either. It still meant they wouldn't get to see each other after tonight and, if anything, could make things worse. He doubted one night would satiate this thirst she'd created inside him.

'Why do we have to label anything? Or spend the whole night discussing terms and conditions, wasting precious time. We could be doing something much more fun.' Evie grabbed his tie and pulled him in for a kiss.

She teased his bottom lip with the tip of her tongue, then tugged it with her teeth, teasing him with a bravado he hadn't realised she possessed.

Perhaps having fun and forgetting their troubles for a while was something they both could do after all. It was clear they both needed it.

Evie was shaking as she walked back into the evening celebrations to retrieve her pashmina and bag, whilst Jake checked them into a room for the night in Reception. The dance floor was crowded now so she was able to slip in and out unnoticed. Thankfully, she didn't run into any of his family members and be forced to explain why they were taking their leave so early in proceedings. She was out of her comfort zone enough without having to add more lies to her conscience.

'Everything okay?' Jake asked when she came to join him at the reception desk. She knew he was asking if she really wanted to do this. To spend the night with him.

She nodded and linked her arm through his. 'Yes. Take me to bed.'

Jake's face darkened, his jaw tightened, and she knew her seduction was working on him. In trying to be the confident, sexy woman who could sleep with someone at a wedding and not think twice about it, she hoped to convince them both it was enough for her.

Of course she wanted more, but Jake had made it clear that wasn't on offer, and she knew she wasn't ready for anything serious either, waiting for that day when it would all come crashing down around her again. At least Jake was upfront about not being the commitment type. If Bailey had done that she would never have risked her heart, or her trust, being broken into a million pieces.

When Jake had danced with her earlier, making her feel special and cherished, it had been like a dream. Until the music ended and she was faced with going back to reality. Something she hadn't been ready to do. She'd thought the whole thing was over too when she'd spilled her guts to Jake outside, never imagining for a second he might have felt the same way. Now they were about to embark on new territory for them both.

'The room's just on the first floor so we…um…don't have too far to go.' Even he seemed a little nervous about what they were about to do as he waved the room key at her.

It occurred to Evie that she didn't have a change of clothes for the morning. Though that probably wasn't something a woman having a casual one-night stand worried about. Chances were that after the wedding she wouldn't be the only one doing the walk of shame in yesterday's clothes.

The short journey to the hotel room was silent, tense, and the atmosphere between them filled with anticipation. They both knew what they were here for, and Evie's pulse was in overdrive. She was sure there was an element of expectation as well as apprehension on both sides and just hoped that chemistry took over, as it tended to do between them, robbing them of common sense and self-consciousness, so that all that mattered was the passion which flared so easily to life when they allowed it.

'I upgraded us. I hope you don't mind,' he said, opening the room door.

It took Evie a second or two to realise he wasn't talking about their relationship.

'Not at all, but, you know, you don't have to seduce me. As I recall, this was my idea.'

Jake didn't have any reason, or need, to try and impress her. He did that anyway and, apart from anything else, it didn't take much to be an improvement from what she was used to with Bailey. His idea of a room upgrade would be booking somewhere that had a hairdryer.

So when she saw the vast suite Jake had booked for the night, complete with king-sized bed, bucket of champagne on ice and a hot tub, she could hardly believe her eyes. Or her luck. If they were only going to have one night together, Jake certainly intended to make it special, one to remember. That thrill of anticipation fizzed in her veins, thinking about what else he had in store for her.

'A hot tub. Now, that is fancy.' She walked over to the square tub sitting at the far end of the room, where there was also a selection of aromatherapy scents, fluffy white towels and robes.

'Not too cheesy?' Jake grimaced, viewing the scene himself for the first time.

'Well, if it is, I don't care. Though I don't have a bathing suit with me…'

'That's okay. For what we'll be doing, you aren't going to need clothes.' He crossed the room towards her in a couple of strides and kissed her so hard and thoroughly it left her breathless.

When he eventually let her up for air, Jake reached down and turned the spa jets on so the tub was filled with inviting bubbles. Evie watched as he undid his tie, unbuttoned his shirt, and cast them aside to reveal his taut, solid body.

She bit her lip, trying to stave off the rush of arousal that coursed through her, when they had such a long night ahead of them. But goodness, he was beautiful. As he popped the button on his fly she couldn't take her eyes off him, until he coughed, forcing her to look at his face instead.

'I think it's your turn,' he said, making no further attempt to undress, apparently waiting for her to give him a show next.

In keeping with the light-hearted, sexy vibe of the moment, Evie kicked her heels off across the room. Then she slowly unzipped the back of her dress, letting it fall at her feet, and reveal her underwear. She'd never thought she'd be here doing this tonight so she thanked her penchant for pretty lingerie. It certainly seemed to have earned Jake's appreciation as he sucked in a breath watching her strip.

'Your turn.' She folded her arms and waited, wearing only her ivory silk bra and panties, and stockings.

At double speed, Jake undid his trousers and let them fall at his feet.

'Next,' he said with a grin.

Evie carefully rolled down her stockings, then held up each foot in turn for Jake to completely remove them. He called her bluff by tugging them off with his teeth and sending her temperature rocketing despite her current lack of clothing. There was something insanely erotic about a man tearing her stockings off with his teeth, the moment only surpassed when he tugged off his boxers and revealed his own impressive arousal.

Evie's cheeks were burning and it wasn't only because it was her turn to strip completely naked, revealing her body to him for the first time. Trying to ignore that little niggle at the back of her head telling her it hadn't been enough to keep Bailey faithful. As if picking up on her insecurity, Jake came to her.

'You're so beautiful.'

He held her close and kissed her so gently, so tenderly, that she forgot all her inhibitions. She could see for herself how much he wanted her.

'Hot tub?' Her voice was thick with desire as she made the suggestion, but she knew if they didn't get in now they never would. She didn't want to waste anything on offer to-night.

'I'll get the champagne.' It was nice to hear that desire reflected back in Jake's voice and know this wasn't necessarily the norm for him either.

Evie watched his perky little butt walk over to the bed to get the bubbly, then lowered her-self down into the hot tub. The pressurised jets of water set to work kneading the knots of tension in her back, which had probably been there for decades. She lay back with a sigh of satisfaction and closed her eyes.

'Now, that's a picture.' Jake slid into the water beside her and handed her a glass of champagne. He dropped a kiss on her lips.

'It's so nice in here. I think I'll stay here for ever.' Evie let the bubbles inside and outside of her glass lift her body and spirits. It was nice to be pampered once in a while and she had to hand it to Jake, who seemed to know exactly what she needed.

'Maybe I'll have one installed in my liv-ing room.' Jake heaved out a groan of plea-sure as he lay back and got his first taste of the bubbles too.

'You do that and you'll never get rid of me.' She'd meant it as a joke, but when the words fell from her mouth she snapped her eyes open to see his reaction, tension immediately taking control of her body again.

Tonight was supposed to be about seizing the moment, not threatening to cling to him for evermore.

'In that case, maybe I'll put one in every room.' His grin was every bit as good at massaging those knots in her muscles as the hot tub.

Another kiss. The taste of champagne from his lips. And a hint that this didn't have to end tonight. A heady mix.

Evie set her glass on the side of the tub and moved so she was straddling Jake's waist, arms around his neck to anchor her in the buoyant water.

'Now I'm definitely putting one in every room,' he growled as she began kissing her way along his collarbone to his neck.

'Hmm-mm? You have a place big enough?'

'You know it.' He buried his face in her neck and thrust his hips up so she knew he wasn't just talking about his house.

He ground himself against her so his arousal was pressed intimately between her thighs. Evie threw her head back in ecstasy, only for Jake to take one of her nipples in his mouth as her breasts bobbed on the water. He seemed determined to drive her crazy, bringing her to the edge of climax every time he touched her.

It was a surreal feeling being so turned on, so wild and spontaneous, when she couldn't remember ever being like this with Bailey. Even in the early days of their relationship they hadn't had this level of passion. Sex had been something expected, scheduled and, if she was honest, nothing to write home about. She'd believed that was how it was supposed to be with 'the one'. Not all about the excitement and ripping one another's clothes off, but sharing a life together. Perhaps that was what had been missing from their relationship. What he'd gone looking for elsewhere, and found with her stepsister.

If she'd known this was what it was supposed to be like maybe she would've ended things herself and not waited around believing a scrap of Bailey's affection was all she was worthy of. Given a chance, she would've swapped all those years thinking she had it all with Bailey for one night with Jake showing her what she'd been missing out on.

Only now she knew, she didn't think she'd be the same woman ever again. Would she find this again with anyone else? What if it was only Jake who could make her feel this way? She had no idea what the future held any more than she knew the answers to those questions. So all she could do was enjoy this while it lasted.

Kissing, petting, the waters swishing around their naked bodies writhing together, they could have been anywhere in the world. A newly married couple on honeymoon, bathing in the warm seas of the tropics, perhaps. Two people in the midst of an illicit affair, snatching whatever time together they could get. That was how intense the moment felt. Except she wouldn't have the luxury of extending her time with Jake beyond tonight.

'Let's take this somewhere more comfortable,' Jake said in a low voice in her ear, bringing goosebumps across her exposed skin.

He got out of the tub, water sluicing down his exquisite naked form, and held out a hand for her. The cold air only sensitised her more. She saw him take in the sight of her rising from the water, lingering on her ever-tightening nipples. Evie grabbed a towel and patted it over her body, giving Jake a glimpse of flesh every now and then, just to see the flash of desire darken his eyes.

By the time they both reached the bed they

were both ravenous for one another. They didn't make it under the covers, their wet, naked bodies rolling around atop as they kissed and fondled, desperate to know each other intimately.

Certainly, Evie wanted to know every inch of him, so she could relive this moment over and over again. She let her hands roam over his chest, so solid and strong beneath her fingertips. Down to his hips, that indent at his waist, and that path of dark hair leading her further into temptation.

She dipped deeper to reach the epitome of his masculinity and grasped him firmly in her hand. There was a satisfaction in hearing him gasp, knowing she had some power over him. She thought it healthier for each partner to have some element of control, in the bedroom at least, if not in the relationship. In hindsight, Bailey had been the one who'd had all the power when they'd been together, playing with her emotions because he knew she loved him, much more than he'd ever cared about her.

Here, with Jake, they were attuned to one another's needs and wants, bringing one another to the brink of ecstasy, then pulling back because they wanted this to last. It wasn't a selfish race to one's own satisfaction. Although that build-up of arousal inside her was becoming too intense to bear much longer.

'Do you have any protection?' she asked, worried something was going to ruin the moment, and at the same time hoping to take that next delicious step with him.

'I think so. Don't go anywhere.' Jake dropped a swift kiss on her lips before going to retrieve his wallet from his jacket pocket and pulling out a condom.

Evie watched as he sheathed himself before coming back to her. Something had changed between them, their previous animal lust to touch and taste one another now replaced with a more tender, loving union. A soft kiss, his gentle touch as he traced the contours of her body with the back of his hand, as though marvelling at her softness and the feel of it against his skin. It didn't lessen the effect he was having on her body and she didn't shy away from letting him know, arching her body up off the bed with a frustrated groan, pressing her softness against the hard ridge of his erection. Until she broke his resolve completely.

Jake slid into her in one smooth movement, filling her full of him, and contentment. He kissed her again and moved slowly inside her, taking control of her body at the tilt of his hips. It felt every bit as deliciously indulgent as relaxing in the hot tub. With every thrust and grunt of effort, he pushed her closer and closer to that release she was desperately reaching for. Waves of bliss rippled through her, the ebb and flow becoming faster, unrelenting, until it was all-consuming. Evie cried out and clung to Jake's shoulders as her climax racked both of their bodies and triggered Jake's own, his guttural groan in her ear telling something of the primal urges lurking behind that gentlemanly exterior. Hearing him lose himself so completely caused her body to shudder again and again, until her extended orgasm left her thoroughly depleted.

How was she ever supposed to go back to real life when she'd just lived out the ultimate erotic fantasy? She had a feeling that being with Jake had changed her for ever, and not just because she seemed to have lost the power in her legs.

This was not where Jake had thought this was going to end up when he'd first walked into Evie's pottery studio. Not only physically, but emotionally too. He'd never expected to meet someone who would make him want to do something as corny as book a room with a hot tub at a wedding, just because he wanted to make their time together special in some small way. So it was more than just about sex. Even though that was exactly what it was supposed to be.

'Are you okay?' Clearly, Evie had noticed him lost in his own thoughts.

'Yeah. Sorry, just trying to get my breath back and form a coherent thought again.' With a few words he was able to change her concerned expression into a smile.

'It was pretty intense, wasn't it?' Evie rolled over onto her side, looking up at him through long dark eyelashes. With her damp hair in tangles around her shoulders, and her cheeks pink from their antics, she looked adorable and sexy all at once.

'Amazing.' He reached over and kissed her again, something he never seemed to tire of doing.

'Do you think anyone has missed us at the reception?'

Jake shook his head. 'If they did, they'd have been up here cheering through the door.'

Evie laughed, a real unselfconscious belly

laugh that only made Jake want to make it happen more often.

'I'm surprised they're not asking you for marks out of ten so they can improve my performance.'

Another chuckle. 'I have absolutely no complaints on that score. Ten out of ten. Would you like me to leave an online review? Five stars. Would come again.'

'That's good to know. Repeat business is always welcome.'

He liked her sense of humour as well as her cheeky grin. That was part of the reason he couldn't seem to simply walk away from her. There was an ease in being with Evie he'd never known before. Probably because he didn't hold back with her. When he'd been with anyone else, he'd kept that emotional distance from the start, wary of getting too close. The way their 'relationship' had started, he'd never had time to erect those barriers. Then he'd got to know her, realised how much they had in common, and by that stage it had been too late. Jake knew that tonight was about more than sex. He'd wanted to explore that connection with Evie before it was too late. Now he had, he knew it was too special just to let her go.

By their own admission, neither of them was ready for anything serious, but perhaps they could find a way to keep this thing going for a while at least.

'Do you mean that?' For a moment he thought Evie could read his thoughts, until he thought back to his last comment about repeat business.

He let out a sigh, wishing this was possible without all the complications. 'I told you I'm not looking to make a commitment.'

'Neither was I. But would it be such a bad thing?'

It was only natural after everything they'd shared for Evie to question his position on relationships. Especially when he was doing the same thing. Jake thought the least he could do was explain why he felt the way he did. If she couldn't handle that, then at least he'd been honest with her.

'You know we moved around a lot when I was a kid… Every time Dad was posted somewhere new, we had to pack up and go. That meant leaving behind all the friends and neighbours and relationships we'd built. I can't tell you how hard that is to do over and over again when you're little and don't really understand why. All you know is that it hurts.'

Evie scooted across the bed and placed her head on his chest and wrapped an arm around his midriff, providing him with that comfort he'd needed all those years ago.

'It must've been so lonely for you, and difficult to start all over again in new places.'

'Yeah. Most of the time Dad wasn't around and sometimes we didn't even speak the language. I was lucky that I had Donna, but we dealt with things differently. Still do. Donna jumps into relationships quickly. She doesn't waste time. Me? I'm the opposite.'

'You hold back.'

'Yes.' Though he knew Evie had come to know him better than most. 'I always leave in the end. Even the one serious relationship I had didn't last because I put myself first. I guess it's my way of protecting myself and I'm not going to change. I know you need someone who is going to be there for you the way Bailey wasn't, and I can't promise that.'

With a hand on his chest, Evie looked up at him. 'I never asked for that. I'm not sure I'll ever trust anyone enough to get into a serious relationship again. Can't we just enjoy this for what it is? Company, amazing sex, and a support group for victims of dysfunctional families.'

Jake chuckled. 'Well, when you put it like that…'

'We both have Christmas to get through. The present-giving, the awkward dinners, the parties… Then there's New Year's. The festive season is a minefield for hermits and workaholics.'

'You think we should carry on with our fake relationship into the New Year?'

The idea had its merits, though there was still that danger of emotional attachment getting wrapped up in the physical aspect of being together. Because he knew he couldn't go back to being together for appearances only. Not when he knew how dynamite they were together in bed.

'Why not? Nobody but us has to know that it's not real. That we're only together to satisfy one another's physical needs, and provide a little support when we have to deal with those awkward family situations. Let's face it, we're not going to see them much after Christmas anyway.'

Apart from Donna, but she wouldn't be surprised when he inevitably ended things with Evie. Even if she probably would be annoyed.

'But if either of us decide to end things before then—'

'No harm done. I think we're getting all the benefits of a real relationship without the hassles that usually come with it. If things start to get messy or complicated, then we'll call it off. We never even have to see each other again.'

Although that wasn't something that sat well with him just now, he could see the benefit of that if somewhere down the line he thought Evie was expecting more from him than they'd agreed on.

'Okay. I think in that case we have a deal.' He held out his hand and Evie shook it. 'Now, I think we should celebrate. Where's that champagne?' He left her temporarily to grab the bottle and brought it back to the bed.

'Now, what are you going to do with that?'

Jake held the cold bottle against her nipple, making her squeal. Then he poured a small amount of liquid into the cleft between her breasts and supped it up. He let a little trickle down into her navel and beyond. Following the river of bubbles with his tongue, he felt Evie tense beneath him. Until he reached that vulnerable spot between her thighs and lapped greedily, and she went limp beneath him.

Jake lifted her legs over his shoulders and plunged deeper inside her, teasing and pleasing her with his tongue. He wanted her to feel as good as he did, perhaps in an attempt to keep this purely about sex for both of them. If he could promise her this every time they were together, then hopefully there would be no need for any emotional involvement at all. It certainly seemed to be the only thing on her mind as she writhed and moaned in ecstasy at his touch. And when Evie's orgasm hit them both he felt like a king.

He told himself this could work if they kept things purely physical. This could be the best Christmas ever, sharing it with Evie, as long as he remembered it wasn't real. Like everything else in his life, it couldn't last for ever.

CHAPTER NINE

'PIZZA'S HERE.' Jake walked into the studio carrying a tower of boxes, just as Evie was setting out the wine and plastic cups for tonight's pupils.

They'd finally scheduled his work's team-building class with Evie, and now they'd finished making their own wobbly pots it was time for refreshments.

'Are you having some, Mr Hanley?' one of his employees asked.

'Of course, and can I get some of that wine too, please?' He set the pizzas down in the middle of one of the workbenches and began to open them so everyone could help themselves.

Evie handed him a glass, assuming he was going to be staying at her place for the night if he wasn't driving. They'd spent most evenings together these past couple of weeks since the wedding. As a rule, they didn't go out much.

That would've seemed too much like dating, she supposed. Not that she was complaining. Her sex life was the best she'd ever had and Jake had made her feel things she hadn't realised possible. As though he'd wakened this wanton inside her who couldn't get enough. She didn't know what would happen to that woman once this thing with Jake came to an end, but she didn't want to think about that when she was having such a good time with him.

Christmas wasn't that far away, time was running out on their 'relationship', and the thought saddened her more than she could have imagined. He'd become such a part of her life that it was going to seem even more empty once he was gone. Even now, watching him share his pepperoni with her dog, she knew she didn't want him to go. As much as she'd promised him, and herself, that she wouldn't become too attached, she hadn't been able to help herself. He'd allowed her to explore a side of herself she hadn't known existed but, more than that, she'd opened up her heart to him. Something she'd never thought she'd be able to do after Bailey.

If things had been different she'd be hoping for more than the casual fling they'd agreed to, but he'd been honest with her from the start that that wasn't what he wanted. It was her own fault if she was left broken-hearted once it was all over. He'd warned her not to fall for him. That bit had been entirely her own doing.

All she could do was keep this time with Jake as a happy memory that would hopefully help her when she did return to the dating pool. He'd made her realise that not all men were like Bailey, and that if she found the right man maybe she could think about settling down again, planning a future that might include marriage and a family. It was a shame that man couldn't be Jake.

'You know, Mr Hanley, you're not as stuffy as I thought you were.'

'No. You weren't afraid to get your hands dirty.'

'Thanks... I think.' Jake accepted the backhanded compliments from his staff in good humour. He'd certainly mucked in tonight, helping set up the wheels with Evie and portion out the clay, as well as helping those struggling with forming the pots.

'And you were so much better than us,' another commented.

'I think he's been having private lessons,'

Donna mischievously added as she sipped her wine.

Although their families knew they were together, they hadn't made any blatant displays of affection in front of his employees. Evie supposed they had no need to, but it highlighted the fact that she still wasn't as much a part of his world as he was of hers.

'I'll fire everyone's pieces in the kiln, and glaze them. After another fire they'll be ready for you to collect in a few weeks. Or Jake... um... Mr Hanley can collect them for you.'

'Yes, I can get them. It's no problem.'

It was on the tip of her tongue to remind him they probably wouldn't be together by then, but resisted. Seeing him again might give her something to look forward to in the New Year.

Once they'd eaten their fill of pizza and downed the wine, the women began to pack up, ready to leave.

'We're heading on to a club if you'd both like to join us?' It was Donna who made the invitation, and Evie wondered how keen the rest really would've been to have their boss trailing along on a night out.

'That's very kind but I've a lot to do here.' Even if she hadn't, she wasn't one for going to clubs and getting drunk. She was more of a homebody. Especially if that meant being at home with Jake's body against hers. Heat infused her skin at the thought of another night of passion ahead with him.

'I think I'll stay and give Evie a hand. Have a good night.' Jake waved them off at the door whilst Evie began collecting all the rubbish for recycling.

'Don't work too hard,' Donna called back with a laugh, no doubt aware of what they'd planned to get up to as soon as everyone had gone.

Jake closed the door and walked back towards her, looking deep in thought. 'Donna's right, you know.'

'About what?' Evie began washing down the potter's wheels and workbenches so the clay didn't have time to harden on them.

'Working too hard. We've both spent all day working, then you tutored all my employees. We need a break. Something other than work and sleep.'

Before she could say anything, he was untying her apron, lifting it over her head and handing her her coat.

'What about Dave?'

'We can walk him back to your place then

head out somewhere. If that's what you'd like?'
He was checking with her, when she couldn't
think of anything nicer to do on a December
evening.

'Anywhere?'

'Within reason.' He added a disclaimer,
probably in case she came up with something
completely hare-brained. Like gliding over
ice, balanced on thin, sharp blades.

'What about ice-skating?' she finally plucked
up the courage to ask after they'd settled Dave
at her place with food and water and his favourite toys to keep him company.

'Ice-skating?' As they passed under the
streetlights she could see the surprised look
on his face.

Well, if this erotic interlude in her life was
going to be over soon, she thought she might
as well add a little romance to the memory.
There couldn't be anything more romantic
than outdoor ice-skating together on a crisp
winter night.

'They set up a rink down in the square every
year. I've always wanted to try it but I thought
I'd look tragic doing it on my own. Plus, I
probably need someone to keep me balanced
since I've never tried it before. What about
you? Do you know how to do it?'

'I did it as a kid, but not for years. I can't say I ever felt the need.'

'And now?' Evie knew she was pushing his boundaries, but it had been his idea to come out, to move beyond the walls of a bedroom, and she was going to take full advantage of it. Perhaps in the hope that he'd begin to see the benefits of being in a real relationship and want to pursue something more with her, instead of ending things when all their Christmas-related commitments were over.

'If that's what you want.' He gave a laugh as if to say he thought it absurd but he'd go along with it for her sake. That was enough for Evie.

Like everything with Jake, she was sure he'd have fun once he was gently persuaded out of his comfort zone. It worked for her too. It occurred to her that they'd both been stuck in their own ways for too long, because they felt safe with the familiar. There was no chance of being hurt if they shut themselves off from the world. But she was beginning to learn there was a lot out there to be enjoyed. She was hoping to convince Jake the same. Then maybe he might be open to the idea of being with someone again too.

'It is, but I'll buy you a drink to say thanks. There's a beer tent somewhere nearby.'

'Ah, alcohol and sharp blades. What a mix.' Despite the mocking tone, Jake went with her to get their skates, and they sat on a bench at the edge of the rink to pull them on.

Evie watched the couples and families out on the ice having fun, wishing to be part of it. There was still that fake element to her time with Jake that wouldn't let her enjoy it completely. As though he was putting on a front to please her, the same way he'd agreed with Donna about putting on the pottery evening for everyone else's sake. He'd seemed to enjoy it in the end, but she wished he could just let himself go for once and really live in the moment. The only time he did that was in the bedroom, and she knew that was because there was no emotional element involved. There was barely even any talking. He felt safe there because she wasn't asking anything more from him than sex. Regardless that she wanted to.

'Don't be such a grouch. Come on.' She stood up, wobbled and almost fell over. Luckily, Jake was at hand to steady her. They weren't even on the ice yet.

'I can see why you wanted me to come. You're a danger to yourself and others.'

'Danger Evie. That's me,' she said with a grin, because this probably was the riskiest thing she'd done in a long time. Apart from agreeing to a casual fling with someone she already knew she cared about.

It was being with Jake that made her want to do crazy things. She wanted to experience new things and challenge herself, because she was happy around him. Safe. She knew that was ironic when their time together had an expiration date coming up, but she wanted to make the most of this feeling for as long as she could. Who knew if it would ever happen again?

Jake stepped onto the ice first, confident and steady. A stark contrast to Evie, who tentatively put one foot out and felt it slide from beneath her.

'It's okay. I've got you,' Jake said in her ear, wrapping an arm around her waist to hold her steady.

He supported her around the ice, just as he'd done from that first night in her studio. Going along with her crazy fake date plan, tackling her crazy family, and staying in her life even after their arrangement was supposed to have ended. It was a shame she hadn't managed to do the same for him, otherwise he might have wanted something more than a fling with her.

Though she supposed she should be grateful for now. This was a start, maybe the end for all she knew, but at least he was happy to be with her when they didn't have an audience. It said he might have some feelings for her beyond the purely physical when he was willing to do this with her. Unless he was just humouring her, and hoping it would ease the pain of their inevitable breakup...

As her mind drifted into not so happy territory, she wobbled and had to grab for the side of the rink. Jake still had hold of her, but she needed that extra support to centre herself again.

'Sorry. I'm holding you back. You probably would've done twenty laps of this place by now if you weren't lumbered with my dead weight.'

She watched the others skating past when she was still slipping and sliding all over the place like a newborn foal trying to find its feet.

In her romantic fantasy they'd be twirling around like Olympic gold medal-winning figure-skaters, instead of Jake trailing her around like a sack of potatoes. It was her fault for building things up in her mind. Again.

'Hey. I'm not here so I can show off. I'm

here to be with you. Okay?' He tilted her chin up and planted a kiss on her lips, most likely a gesture of comfort and support, but, as it always did, it soon turned into something more. Until Evie felt herself blush, knowing they were putting on a very public display.

'We're going to get thrown out if we keep doing that.'

'Good. Then maybe we can get out of here and go back to your place.' The look he gave her, and the promise in his eyes, was enough to melt her heart right along with the ice beneath them.

More than that, it was the first time he'd kissed her like that in front of anyone. Usually they did that in private, where no one could see. It marked a change in their relationship, as had this venture out, and Evie couldn't prevent her heart swelling with hope. Maybe, just maybe, Jake was opening his life up to her too.

'What about that drink first?' As much as she was looking forward to their time in bed, as she always did, it would be nice to be with him in the real world for a little bit longer.

'Are we done here?'

'I think so. It didn't turn out quite the romantic experience I expected.'

It wasn't Jake's fault. He'd done everything right, but if she attempted to stumble her way any further around the ice she was in serious danger of landing face first. That definitely wasn't going to impress him.

'Oh? I didn't know that's what we were doing. Am I supposed to be romancing you?'

Jake escorted her back so she could change into more stable footwear and she wished she could change into a more stable human being at the same time. Then she wouldn't say such cringe-worthy stuff that caused Jake to look at her with suspicion. As if she'd tricked him into doing something awful.

'That's not what I meant. It's just…in all the Christmas films the couples are instant skating experts, tripping around hand in hand, as though they're not frozen to the bone. Not flailing around like a seal trying to make it onto dry land.'

'It was your first time. You did well.' Regardless of his praise, there was something hollow in Jake's words. The set of his jaw was not the usual smile she'd come to expect when they had quality time together.

Evie had a sense that she'd stuffed things up. That by making this into something other than an evening out, it had spoiled the arrangement. To assert some damage control, she led him over to the faux log cabin selling hot drinks.

'A beer, wasn't it? They do that hot German beer. I think I'll try a mulled cider. Do you want one of those instead? It might warm us up.'

'Just a beer, thanks.'

Yeah, he definitely wasn't happy.

'You know, that was just a joke back there. I didn't mean anything by it. I'm not trying to force you into a relationship you don't want, Jake.'

She decided it was better to tackle the subject head-on rather than let it fester between them. Perhaps if she and Bailey had talked more, she would have realised something was wrong long before she'd caught him with Courtney.

She'd been so wrapped up in the idea of settling down, having kids, creating the family she hadn't had in such a long time, that she'd ignored any problems, convinced herself all was well between them because she didn't want to lose everything. Looking back now, comparing what she'd had with Jake these past weeks to how things had been with Bailey for years, there was a vast difference. Perhaps she'd latched onto Bailey long after the initial spark between them had gone because she wanted that cosy family dream. She didn't want to make the same mistake with Jake.

'I know. Don't worry.' He smiled, but she still wasn't convinced by it.

Her worst fears were confirmed when she asked if he was ready to head back to her place.

'You know, it's been a long day. I might just head home tonight, if that's okay?'

'Sure,' she said brightly, even though she was dying inside. Her eagerness to push him into something he wasn't ready for was driving him away. The best she could do now was give him the space he needed and hope it was enough.

Gentleman that he was, he insisted on walking her back but he didn't come in, not even to see the dog.

'Thanks for tonight.' She hovered on the doorstep, feeling as though they'd just come to the end of a very awkward first date when it was obvious there wasn't going to be a second one.

'I had fun. I'll call you tomorrow.' The goodbye kiss was brief and perfunctory, not at all what Evie had become accustomed to.

''Bye.' She waved him off, her smile forced and her heart heavy. It seemed the final countdown had begun. If he was already stewing over being inadvertently romantic, they'd be lucky to see Christmas together.

Jake couldn't concentrate. The screen full of charts and figures was a blur today, his mind preoccupied with thoughts of Evie and last night, knowing he'd spoiled their evening. It had been his idea to go out and do something other than fall into bed, taking their relationship into the real world, where they weren't putting on an act for anyone else, simply enjoying each other's company. Or at least they had been, until he'd freaked out at the mere mention of romance.

Of course ice-skating at Christmas was romantic, and he shouldn't blame Evie for pointing that out. But it had been so long since he'd been in anything resembling a romantic relationship he'd panicked. Evie knew the score. This thing between them was temporary and they didn't have much time left together. It wasn't her fault he'd started to have feelings for her, and run away—his usual self-defence mechanism.

It had all felt so normal, fitting in with the other couples and families out on the ice. Holding her in his arms. That was what had caused him so much concern. That it was becoming the norm, and he'd been content to keep pretending things between them were still casual. The trouble was, he didn't want to stop seeing her. As long as she wasn't expecting more than he was prepared to give, he hoped they could still enjoy the time they had left together.

His phone rang, Evie's number flashing up on the screen. This was the moment he had to decide if he wanted to keep on seeing her, or end things now before someone got hurt. He snatched the phone up without a second thought.

'Hello?'

'Hi. I hope I'm not disturbing you?' He could hear the uncertainty in her voice about contacting him and he was sorry he was the one who'd put it there. Evie had had enough of being made to feel uncomfortable in her life through no fault of her own and he didn't want to be another one on that list.

'Not at all. What can I do for you?' It wasn't as though he was getting any work done anyway.

There was a sigh on the other end of the phone, as though she was building up to ask him a favour and really didn't want to. 'I was wondering if you were free for an hour or two to give me a hand with something.'

'Sure. What is it?'

'I need to pick up my Christmas tree. I swear I'm not trying to force you into some Christmas tree romance fantasy. I just need a strong pair of hands and a vehicle to help me with transporting it. Ursula is off for a couple of days and I don't want to leave it much longer or there's no point in getting a tree so close to Christmas Day.'

Overexplaining why she needed his help so much made him feel even worse that she thought she couldn't ask him for a favour without him turning it into a big deal.

'It's fine. I'm free now if you're ready to go?'

'That would be great, Jake. Thank you.'

'I'll see you soon.' He hung up with an increasing sense that things had changed irrevocably between them, and he only had himself to blame.

Jake closed down his laptop, grabbed his jacket and headed for the door. Running straight into Donna outside.

'Are you off again? You really are a changed man.' She walked away, shaking her head, a smile playing on her lips.

Leaving Jake frowning. She was right. Up until Evie had come into his life, he wouldn't have left the office for anything, work his sole focus. It was a big change for someone who was only supposed to be in his life on a temporary basis. If he'd changed, made room in his life for something other than work, then what was going to happen to him once the relationship ended? Everything he'd been afraid of since he was a child. Of being hurt, being lonely, and with a great big hole in his life where the people who meant most to him in the world used to be.

'Sorry about this,' Evie apologised the moment she got into the passenger seat.

'It's fine. Though I did take time to change into something more suitable for the occasion.' His red and black plaid shirt, worn jeans and tan boots did manage to raise a smile.

'Me too.' She clapped her gloved hands together, the same pale pink as her soft wool sweater and bobble hat. Even though they weren't going to be trekking through an actual tree farm, she was wearing jeans and boots too. At least they were dressed appropriately for any unexpected snowfall. It was certainly cold enough.

'I'm not sure if I'm the big city executive about to lose the girl, or the charming home-body who gives her her happy-ever-after, like in all of those cheesy Christmas films.'

Evie slid an amused gaze across at him. 'I don't know, but I never took you as the type to watch sentimental Christmas movies.'

Busted.

'Donna and Mum like them. I've caught a glimpse every now and then. I know the formula.'

That had been the one constant around the season. From November, those movies were always on the TV at home, no matter which part of the world they were living in at the time. They were a safe romantic fantasy where no one got hurt and they all lived happily ever after so he hadn't minded watching them. It probably helped that their mum had always made them hot chocolate with marshmallows so they could really get in the Christmas mood. He found something comforting even now about having them on in the background when he was at home. Not that he would admit that to anyone…

'Uh-huh.' Evie clearly wasn't convinced by his explanation, but at least the subject of his guilty pleasure had broken the ice between them.

'Are you telling me you don't watch them?'

'Not any more. Once you've had your heart so spectacularly broken it's difficult to watch things like that without crying a river or, you know, wishing a meteorite would hit Snow Falls, or wherever these annoying happy people live.'

'You should watch yourself, Evie. Hanging around with me is making you cynical.'

'Ach, I'm only joking. I love Christmas. Probably more than I ever loved Bailey. I'm beginning to wonder if I only stayed with him as long as I did because I thought he could give me the family I always wanted.'

Evie stared out of the window, and the longing in her voice would've melted most people's hearts. For Jake, however, it was another red flag.

'I didn't think you wanted another serious relationship.'

'I didn't. Maybe it's the season, and seeing everyone else with their little ones, but it's made me think I might be ready to start over with someone else. I always thought I'd have children and be content as a wife and mother. I know I've got my own business and that's great, but I just feel as though something's missing. I'm not saying it's going to happen any time soon, but I'm still hoping that some day I'll have the family I didn't have when I was growing up. It's not too much to ask, is it?'

It was for him.

'I can understand that. I'm sure you'll make a great mother.' Unfortunately, that was the opposite of what he wanted in the future.

'What about you? Didn't you ever want a family?'

'I can't say it's anything I've ever really considered. I've never been with anyone long enough for it to be an issue. In that respect, I suppose the answer's no.'

With his reluctance to get close to anyone, it wouldn't be fair on a child, or its mother. He was always going to be holding back, and if his father had taught him one thing it was that a child needed love. Something he found hard to give freely.

With both having voiced their very different views of the future, they lapsed into silence. It was clear they had no long-term future ahead, but they'd always known that. So why did Jake feel as though his supposed impenetrable heart had just taken a hit?

They pulled up to the Christmas tree lot, where the freshly cut spruces and firs were waiting for new homes.

'You know you can get plastic trees you can use every year, and they're cheaper.'

Jake had never had the pleasure of a real tree at Christmas. Though he realised he now sounded like his dad, who'd insisted they made too much mess, as well as being a waste of money. Jake wondered if that was the problem, or the fact that it might have brought the family some degree of pleasure, which it seemed he did his best to stamp out.

Evie held out one of the green branches. 'Just smell that. It smells like Christmas. You don't get that with a fake tree, and they're better for the environment. For every one chopped down here, another one is planted in its place.'

Jake inhaled the fresh scent and he had to agree the real thing was much better than the fake stuff.

'Maybe I'll have a look too. It might be nice to have a small one in the office.'

Donna would appreciate it, and it might brighten the place up a little. Perhaps a little of Evie's Christmas spirit was rubbing off on him.

Evie wasn't listening, wandering off to find

a tree that was 'just right'. There was an incredible sense of whimsy about her which kept her childlike and adorable. Whoever got to spend his life with her would be very lucky.

He watched her interact with those around her, a cheery greeting to a stranger, every dog that went past getting treated to some attention, and her out-of-tune singing along with the Christmas tunes blaring out from nearby speakers. Evie was a ray of sunshine on this cold and dreary winter afternoon.

As she passed a young father struggling with a toddler in the midst of a temper tantrum, instead of walking on by as most had already done, casting a dirty look, she stopped and knelt down.

'Who's making all this racket?'

At the sound of her voice, the little girl paused her histrionics, though still refused to take her father's hand.

'She doesn't want to go without a tree but I think they're all too big for our flat,' the dad sighed.

'Oh, sweetie. It's not Daddy's fault. Maybe you'll find one somewhere else,' Evie soothed.

'I want one here,' the little diva insisted with a stamp of her foot.

'Maybe if you're a really good girl and take

Daddy's hand we can find you a really special tree, just for you.' She gave the harassed father a wink, and both he and Jake watched on, intrigued, as Evie walked over to the man selling the trees.

The child too seemed curious. Enough to take her father's hand without a further fight and follow Evie.

Jake hid a smirk as he saw her charm the salesman into giving her what looked like the broken top or offcut of a full-size tree. With a little more persuasion, she managed to secure a small plastic pot and a handful of soil to plant it. It wasn't more than a couple of small branches sticking up out of the pot but when she handed it to the little girl it might as well have been a ten-foot Norwegian Spruce.

'Now, this is a very special tree. You have to look after it very carefully. Make sure you water it, and if you're a very good girl for your daddy, maybe he'll let you decorate it all by yourself.'

The child looked up hopefully at her father. 'I promise, Daddy.'

'Good girl. I'm sure we have some tinsel and lights you can put on it.' The dad took the tree from Evie and gently delivered it into his daughter's open hands.

'Thank you so much,' he said with genu-ine appreciation.

Jake felt a little twinge of something un-comfortable at watching the interaction. Per-haps if he hadn't been here this scene might have played out differently. Though he wasn't aware of the man's circumstances, if he was single, this would've been the perfect meet-cute. A ready-made family for Evie. Every-thing she wanted.

Jake's choice of clothes today didn't really matter. He was the city guy in a suit about to lose the girl to a hometown boy.

Okay, so he was being a tad melodramatic, Evie was just being her usual kind self, but it was obvious she was born to be a mother, and she was going to make someone a fantastic wife. It just couldn't be him. Even if it wasn't this guy with his daughter, there was going to be someone else who could give Evie ev-erything she longed for. But marriage, babies, a family…just weren't for him. That meant sharing his life completely with other people, and he wasn't ready for that. If ever.

Marriage and children were the ultimate commitments of himself, and his heart. If it didn't work out, as had been his experience so far in life, he knew he wouldn't recover. It would be too great a loss for him to bear, and he'd been hurt too much in the past.

Evie had helped him open his heart a little bit to let her in, and whilst he liked what they had now, by her own admission, it wasn't going to be enough for her long-term. Though he'd sworn he didn't want a serious relationship, the thought of not having her in his life was already causing him pain. Jake was beginning to wonder if he had finally found someone who made him want to make room in his life for her. Only time would tell if he was strong enough, and willing to do so. Unfortunately, the countdown was already on.

CHAPTER TEN

'THANK YOU SO much for doing this, Jake.'

'I forgot you didn't live on the ground floor when I volunteered,' he huffed, carrying the heavy end of the tree up the stairs to Evie's flat.

She might have been better thanking him when he could breathe again and was in better form after they'd discovered the lift was broken. Despite his assistance today, she could sense a distance between them that hadn't been there before. It wasn't just about last night either.

Earlier, at the Christmas tree lot, when she'd interacted with the father and daughter, she'd felt a little pang. The scene had reminded her of Christmases spent with her own father, just the two of them getting ready for the big day. It had made her realise that she did want that some day, with her own family. Something she was never going to have with Jake. He'd made it clear having children was not on his agenda. However, she was already having feelings for him, and if they had very different ideas of the future it seemed as though a relationship with him was doomed. By carrying on, pretending otherwise was just going to cause more heartbreak.

Jake had backed away when she'd even hinted at something more, and today had been a reality check. Despite her growing feelings for him, she was beginning to think he couldn't be the man for her and she was only breaking her own heart by pretending otherwise.

'Can I make you a hot chocolate?' she offered once they had it in situ in her living room after a lot of huffing, puffing and swearing, thinking she should offer some kind of thanks for inconveniencing him even though she would prefer to put some space between them.

'I should probably get back to work.'

'Of course. Thanks again for your help.'

'Listen, Evie, about last night… I'm sorry about bailing on you.'

Hearing him raise the subject and knowing the conversation she needed to have made Evie's insides lurch.

'Don't worry about it. I know that sort of thing isn't your scene and I shouldn't have pushed you into it.'

'I've been thinking a lot about us today…'

Evie took a deep breath. He was giving her the perfect opportunity to get out now before she completely lost her heart to him.

'Me too. I know the plan was to keep seeing one another over Christmas, but I think it's pretty obvious we're very different people. We want different things, and I don't see the point in pretending otherwise.'

'Oh.'

He looked stunned. Probably because she'd beaten him to the punch.

'We did what we set out to do. We were there for each other when we needed it and we had fun. But I think we're just putting off the inevitable by continuing this. It's probably time we both got back to real life.'

The nausea was overwhelming now, because she didn't want it to end. She didn't want to lose Jake now, when she was just beginning to feel like herself again, but waiting for him to feel differently about her, and about what he wanted in life, seemed like a futile exercise. Though a broken heart definitely hadn't been on her Christmas list.

'If that's what you want.' It was a verbal shrug, as if it didn't mean anything to him. He wasn't putting up a fight, simply accepting the end. Likely because he'd come to the same conclusion, albeit for different reasons.

If it was really so easy for him to move on then he clearly didn't feel the same way about her as she did about him. Because the thought of never seeing him again was devastating. But she wasn't going to humiliate herself again by begging him to love her. She'd invested too long in a relationship with a man who didn't want her before, and she wasn't about to do it again.

'I'd rather leave things on good terms now than wait until our differences really start to make themselves known.'

'I guess...'

'What will you tell the family?' She was asking questions, faking her acceptance of the situation, but she was feeling kind of numb.

'Nothing, unless they ask. It won't come as a surprise even if I do say we've split up.'

Evie felt foolish to have imagined a rapport with his family, believing that anyone would care that she was no longer part of their lives. Clearly, she was the only one who'd thought there was a possibility that this could have been a long-term thing.

'Okay. Then I guess this is it. Thanks for walking into the studio that night.' Her voice cracked and she stopped herself from saying anything else.

'Thanks for everything, Evie.'

Jake moved as if to offer a hug, but she didn't want that. She knew if he touched her she'd break down and never want to let him go.

Instead, she ducked past him and opened the front door. 'I'll let you get back to work. Have a good Christmas, Jake.'

He hesitated in the doorway as if to say something more, then simply gave a lopsided smile and walked away.

She felt numb. As he disappeared out of sight down the stairs it felt like a death, the loss was so great. The death of her hopes and dreams, and the misplaced belief that she'd found 'the one'. If she couldn't find happiness with Jake, she knew she'd never find it with anyone.

'I can't believe it's Christmas Day tomorrow already.' Donna was perched on Jake's desk when he came back from making himself a coffee. He'd been in work at six a.m., as he had every day since he'd walked out of Evie's apartment. It was either that or lie staring at the ceiling for another couple of hours, wondering what had happened between them, and he was sure he knew every crack and fleck of paint on it by now.

'It's just another day as far as I'm concerned.' He'd probably be in work like every other day, but he didn't want to tell her that and have her tut and roll her eyes at him in despair. He was feeling low enough at the moment.

'I assumed you'd have special plans with Evie, like Mum and Gary do for their first Christmas together. I mean, *I* wouldn't want to spend Christmas Day in a hotel, but as long as they're happy. So are you not seeing Evie at all?' She lifted the pen from his desk, not making eye contact, and started doodling on his desk pad.

Jake took it off her and set it down again, hoping she hadn't seen him wince when she'd mentioned Evie. 'Nope.'

'Are you two not together any more?' It was a fishing exercise, but he was just surprised she hadn't quizzed him about his love life before now.

'Nope.'

He didn't want to get into it. There was no burning desire to hear her tell him how stupid he was to let her go out of his life, because he already knew it. He felt it every time he went home to an empty house and bed, and when he had no one to have a laugh with at the end of a difficult day.

Evie had taken him by surprise when she'd told him she didn't want to see him again, because he'd been on the verge of telling her the opposite. That he wanted to commit to something beyond Christmas. However, he hadn't argued with her reasoning. It had become clear that she was looking to settle down, and he wasn't the man who could offer her that stability. He'd opened his heart to her, but with such differing views of their future, they would never have survived. In the end he'd thought it best to go along with her decision rather than prolong the pain.

Except he didn't feel any better not having her in his life any more. He hadn't realised the misery he'd be in simply by walking away.

'That's a shame. She was nice.'

'Yes, she was.' He carried on typing, even though he couldn't see the words on the screen clearly.

'There's no chance—'

'No.' He cut her off before she even asked about a reconciliation. He'd clearly underestimated the impact she'd made on him and how much he'd miss her. However, how he felt about her didn't change the reasons they'd had to part. It would've been selfish of him to keep things going, knowing he couldn't fulfil those dreams she had for the future.

'You could come around to mine. We'll make dinner and put on some of those Christmas films you love.' She was teasing him, but nothing could raise his spirits, knowing he could've been spending the day with Evie if only he hadn't been so cowardly.

'We'll see.' He had no intention of listening to the pity and recriminations, but it would be enough of an answer to hopefully get rid of his sister in the meantime.

'I don't want you to spend the day on your own, wallowing.'

He was about to ask her how she knew he was wallowing, but instead found himself asking, 'How do you do it, Donna? How do you pick yourself up after a breakup and start all over again?'

This wasn't his first breakup, of course, but usually he was the one to end things and he didn't dwell too much on the person he'd had to let down. Other than his ex, of course, but this was different. He'd opened up to Evie in a way he had never done with anyone else. Now it felt as though he'd lost a part of himself with her. As if those parts of himself which he'd shared with her were hers for ever, and instead of learning and evolving he'd fallen back into his old ways, completely shutting down emotionally rather than dealing with his feelings. Telling her what she meant to him.

He was opening himself up now to Donna for another lecture, and he half expected her to point out the obvious, that this felt different because Evie had been more than a passing fancy.

'I cry, I rant and rave, then I realise that I wasn't with the right person. Otherwise, they would've fought harder for me, for us. So I dust myself off and put myself out there, until some day the right man will find me.'

He knew his sister was a romantic, but he'd never had her down as an optimist. The exact opposite of his outlook. If he lived the way she did, he would've told Evie how he felt, asked her to give him a chance. Maybe even some day contemplating marriage and starting a family, and hoping they'd live happily ever after.

Now he was beginning to wonder what was wrong with that. There was nothing to lose for someone who'd already had their heart broken and didn't know how he'd ever live without the woman he'd come to love. He realised now that was how strong his feelings had been for Evie. That was the reason he'd panicked and run as soon as she'd given him an out. As if he could shut down those feelings and go back to life the way it had been before he'd walked into that pottery studio. These past days without her had proved that wasn't possible.

He didn't know if marriage and children were something he wanted right now, but he did want to be with Evie. Only time would tell if he'd ever be ready for that kind of commitment but, as Evie had reminded him, she'd never asked him for that. All she'd wanted was to be with him. She hadn't tried to label anything, or catastrophise the future, but simply tried to live in the moment with him.

Maybe it was about time to see where those feelings took him. And share them with Evie. If she still didn't want him at least he would know he'd tried. He might be pleasantly surprised, and anything had to be better than this torturous limbo he was in without Evie.

He got up from his desk. 'Donna, tell everyone to go home.'

'What? Really?'

'Yes. It's Christmas Eve. Everyone should be with their loved ones. Including me.' He just hoped it wasn't too late for this fake commitment-phobe to prove how he really felt.

'It looks as though it's just you and me for Christmas, Dave.'

Evie tossed the dog a piece of the turkey she'd brought with her to the studio. She'd spent the evening at home cooking it in the hope the smell at least would put her in a festive mood. To no avail. All she could think about still was Jake, and how they should've been spending tomorrow together. How they should've been spending every Christmas together, but self-preservation had caused her to push him away before she fell any further for him.

Instead of cosying up with Jake in a Christmas card scene, she was talking to her dog in her cold pottery studio on Christmas Eve. She'd had a last-minute booking for a private lesson. Any other time she would've turned it down, but she needed the money, as well as the distraction.

The knock on the door signalled her student's arrival.

'Come in,' she called, busying herself with setting up the wheel for the lesson.

She had her back to the door when her guest walked in.

'Just hang your coat up and put an apron on. You can make yourself a cup of tea if you want whilst I'm setting up.'

'Do you have any hot chocolate?'

The sound of Jake's voice froze her to the spot. Until she heard his footsteps crossing the floor and she turned before he could reach her.

'What are you doing here?'

'I'm here for my pottery lesson.'

It took her a moment to register what he was saying.

'You booked the private session?'

He at least looked shamefaced as he nodded, accepting that he'd lied about his name at least.

'I wanted to see you and I thought it was the best way to know for sure where you'd be, and that I could speak to you in private.'

Her initial shock and delight at seeing him again quickly changed into something more painful. By turning up here when she was doing her best to get over him he was making her go through that rejection and loss all over again when he left.

'Well, I've been paid to give a pottery lesson, but if that's not why you're here then I'm going home. It's Christmas Eve and I have better things to do than be the object of ridicule.'

She didn't, but he didn't have to know that. Up until recently her plans had been to spend the day with him, and she hadn't been able to face the fact she'd be alone instead. She hadn't even told her stepmother they'd split up, afraid she'd be forced to go there for Christmas dinner and be ridiculed over her single status in front of a smug Courtney and Bailey. So her current plans simply included sharing a turkey dinner with her dog. None of which Jake needed to know.

When she rolled down her sleeves and prepared to pack away her equipment again, he quickly donned an apron and took a seat at the wheel.

'Can we at least talk while we work?'

'That's up to you, but you might need to concentrate unless you want to end up with clay in your lap.' She slapped a ball of clay in the centre of the wheel, splattering him with wet residue.

'I wanted to see how you were doing.'

'Fine.' Evie pushed the accelerator pedal down, forcing him to focus on the clay and stop it from flying off the wheel. She didn't have to play nice when he was deliberately goading her simply by being here. There was absolutely no reason for him to do this other than to watch her suffer.

'Good. Good.'

'Remember, you have to raise the clay up, then flatten it.' Pretty much the way her heart felt, she thought to herself, wondering why he'd come to torture her.

Annoyingly, he followed her instructions perfectly. 'Like this?'

'Yes. Now, we need to open up that divot in the middle.' She could feel him looking at her and she did her best to ignore it, not wanting her soft heart to give in if she should lock eyes with him. He had no business being here, or having an effect on her heart.

'I'm sorry.'

The words made her and the clay wobble, so she had to pull things back and re-centre everything.

'Just concentrate on the clay,' she warned.

'I'm not here for the clay.'

It was difficult to maintain that pretence of indifference when her hands were on his and he was practically begging her to look at him.

'Well, that's what you've paid for.' She dipped a sponge and squeezed the water over the clay.

'I'm sorry, Evie. I should have fought harder for us.'

'Okay.' She wasn't going to argue with him on that score, but neither did it change anything.

Jake gave up all pretence that he was here for a lesson, turning around so she was now trapped between his legs. If her heart wasn't beating so fast she thought she'd pass out, she might have made a joke about that.

'I had come that day to ask if we could make a proper go of things. But when you pointed out that we wanted different things and it would inevitably come between us, I took the easy way out.'

'And has being apart been easy for you, because it sucked for me.' She offered a half smile, afraid to believe that he had real feelings for her in case she got hurt again.

He shook his head. 'No. Apparently, feelings don't go away just because they're inconvenient.' The way he looked at her now, so open and vulnerable, Evie had to stop pretending she didn't care deeply for him too.

'So now what? What's changed? I want security, and a family some day. You don't. I can't see how we can reconcile those differences.'

'All I can tell you is that I've fallen for you, Evie. Maybe it took you ending things to make me admit that. Afraid if I didn't tell you now, I'd lose you for ever. You have to understand that I'm still traumatised by my childhood. I was forced to leave people I came to care about so often I learned to shut myself off emotionally, to stop it hurting so much. Somehow, you managed to break through that barrier.'

'I'm sneaky that way,' she joked, trying to make light of the situation because she was afraid to take it too seriously just yet.

'I know I want a future with you. I just need to know if you feel the same way. I've missed you, Evie.'

That simple statement was enough to break her. He was putting everything on the line for her. Fighting for them. Treating her as though she was the most important thing in his life, and no one had done that since her father passed away. That didn't mean she wasn't afraid of investing her heart, and her future, in Jake again.

'You know the damage Bailey did to me, and putting my trust in a relationship with you is a big deal for me.'

'I know. I was afraid of making a commitment to you because I knew that meant leaving myself vulnerable again too if things didn't work out between us.'

'And now?'

'I'm more afraid of not having you in my life. I don't know what the future holds, but I do know that I want to be with you, Evie.'

'How do I know that anything's going to change? You're not the only one afraid of getting hurt again.'

'I've taken some time off work. I want to spend Christmas and New Year together, and focus on us. I'll do whatever it takes to have you back in my life.'

Already won over, Evie walked further in between his legs. 'Anything?'

'I'm yours completely.'

She knew Jake wouldn't make such a gesture if he didn't mean what he said. He was willing to take a chance on them in the hope of nurturing something special, and she knew she wanted the same.

'I'm yours too. I was from the moment you agreed to be my fake date.' Now she was ready to embrace the real thing.

Jake kissed her and she knew without doubt she'd finally found someone willing to give her the love she'd always deserved.

EPILOGUE

'THAT'S THE TREE almost finished,' Evie said, taking a step back to admire her handiwork, though Jake had paid for it to be delivered this year from the Christmas tree farm.

'Almost?' Jake wandered in from the kitchen, where he'd been making dinner as he did most evenings after work. This was their time together, both learning that work ended once they came home. The home he'd invited her and Dave to share with him at the start of the year, showing how invested he was in their relationship.

She knew what a big step that was for him, and hoped the next stage of their life together wasn't going to ruin what they had.

'I need the angel to go on the top. Can you do it?' She handed Jake the precious angel her father had left to her, once belonging to her mother. A real family heirloom she hoped to hand down to the next generation some day.

Jake gave her a puzzled look but took it from her and gently placed it on the top. 'There. Is that okay?'

'Perfect. I'd have done it myself but I don't want to stretch up that far. It's early days but I don't want to take any chances.'

He frowned again at her ramblings. 'Any chances of what?'

'Doing anything that might hurt the baby.'

She'd spent days worrying and wondering how to break the news to him, and in the end she couldn't find any right way of doing it. There was nothing that was going to prepare him for an unexpected pregnancy, and she only hoped that their relationship was strong enough to survive it when he'd made it clear he hadn't intended starting a family.

She watched his face, waiting to interpret his expression, her breath caught in her throat. This past year together had been wonderful. He was so attentive and loving she didn't know why either of them had been so worried about committing to one another. Now she was worried that three in the relationship would prove too much for him to cope with.

'Baby?'

She bit her lip as she nodded.

'We're going to have a baby?'

'Yes. I know we hadn't planned on a family. At least not yet, but I don't see why this has to change anything. I think you'll make a great father.'

Jake was nothing like his own, and was always present. Evie was sure he would be the same for their child.

However, his reaction when it came was worse than she could ever have imagined. He simply turned and walked out of the room. Panic rose inside her, the fear that she'd be left homeless and having to raise this baby on her own very real. It wasn't as though she had her family to support her when she'd distanced herself more than ever since last Christmas. She hadn't needed their toxicity in her life when she'd had Jake's love and support. Now she was going to be completely on her own.

'Jake? Can't we talk this through?'

To her relief, he strode back into the room.

'I'm sorry this happened, Jake, but I'm sure we can survive this. We're strong.'

'I know, that's why I went to get this. I was going to wait until Christmas, but I don't want you to think I'd only ask you because you were pregnant. I was already planning this.' He produced a small velvet box and opened it to reveal a beautiful emerald-cut diamond ring.

Evie blinked at it, then Jake, not knowing what to say.

Then he got down on one knee. 'Evie Kerrigan, I love you. You're the family I never knew I needed, and now this baby is just the icing on the cake. Will you marry me?'

She had no reason to hesitate. 'Yes. Of course I'll marry you. I love you.'

Jake slid the ring onto her finger and she knew they had a happy future together to look forward to. Her fake date had turned out to be her Prince Charming after all.

* * * * *

*If you enjoyed this story,
check out these other great reads
from Karin Baine*

Highland Fling with Her Boss
Pregnant Princess at the Altar
Festive Fling with the Surgeon
Midwife's One-Night Baby Surprise

All available now!